Friend,

Thank you for taking the time to read these humble thoughts each day just as if you were reading letters written directly to you from God.

These are not inspired or without error, but have come from thoughts God has impressed upon my own heart at times, and are based off His scripture.

I hope they speak to you in some special way, and give you just a glimpse of how much He truly cares for you. May they drive you to seek Him passionately through His Word. He's just crazy about you!

Blessings,

Kristi

Day 1

*"But blessed is the one who trusts in the Lord, whose
confidence is in him. They will be like a tree planted by the
water that sends out its roots by the stream. It does not fear
when heat comes; its leaves are always green. It has no
worries in a year of drought and never fails to bear fruit."*
Jeremiah 17:7-8

Dear Child,

Today as you go about your day, I'm asking you to trust
me. Never forget that I go before you, so be not afraid for
my plans are solid. Your faith may be weak, but I am
strong! I will do amazing things in your presence, if you
simply trust me. Look at the tree by the water. It does not
fret or wither; it is not swept away by the current. No, it
puts down strong roots—roots that dig deep into the fertile
soil. Be like that tree by allowing your spiritual roots to run
deep into my Word. I know there are times you feel
overwhelmed by the things of this world but find your rest
in me. I have overcome the world and still have much work
for you to do. Let me lead you, for my yoke is easy and my
burden light. Together, you and I can do this!

Your Heavenly Daddy

Day 2

*"'For I know the plans I have for you,' declares the Lord,
'plans to prosper you and not to harm you, plans to give
you hope and a future. Then you will call on me and come
and pray to me, and I will listen to you. You will seek me
and find me when you seek me with all your heart.'"*
Jeremiah 29:11-13

Dear Child,

You begin each day like a blank piece of paper. I
continuously write words of life onto your page—words
you can live by. Every day, every moment, I am pouring
into you my truths. I know the plans I have for you; plans
that I established from the beginning of time, carefully
created specifically with you in mind. It is your job to listen
and obey. I don't always make these plans obvious. You
must search for them like fine jewels. How do you do that?
Stay close to me and I will guide you and direct your paths.
I know it will seem difficult sometimes, but know that
through the process of searching, your faith is being
strengthened. Child, simply draw near to me, and I will be
found. Hold tightly to my words for they are like apples of
gold in settings of silver. Their cost is priceless. Trust me,
for I am trustworthy!

Your Heavenly Daddy

Day 3

"Now if we are children, then we are heirs—heirs of God and co-heirs with Christ, if indeed we share in his sufferings in order that we may also share in his glory."
Romans 8:17

Dear Child,

Draw near to me and listen. Never forget that you are a child of the King! Those who have surrendered their heart to me are crowned heirs, sharing in all the riches of my Kingdom, therefore, because of my sacrifice for you, you are royalty! You no longer follow the ways of the defeated one, for I have planted within you a seed of righteousness. You are precious to me and I will guide you wherever you go. The paths I lead you on, though difficult at times, will prove my love and devotion to you, but will also strengthen your love and devotion to me. I will never leave you nor forsake you. Instead I will lead the way. Listen to, search for, and seek after me. I will prove myself faithful.

Your Heavenly Daddy

Day 4

"Hear my cry, O God; listen to my prayer. From the ends of the earth I call to you, I call as my heart grows faint; lead me to the rock that is higher than I. For you have been my refuge, a strong tower against the foe." Psalm 61:1-3

Dear Child,

Today, put your focus on me. There are so many distractions vying for your attention, but I am the one you should set your thoughts on. When fears arise, simply say my name. Not only will I be near you, but peace like a river will invade your soul. When you are feeling overwhelmed by your circumstances, turn to Me. Together we can sort through the unnecessary clutter and get you back on the right path. Keep your focus always on me. I am your Rock, your point of solitude. Seek refuge in Me and I will shelter you from the storms of life. I am for you!

Your Heavenly Daddy

Day 5

"Because of the LORD's great love we are not consumed, for his compassions never fail. They are new every morning; great is your faithfulness." Lamentations 3:22-23

Dear Child,

Today is a new day—embrace it. In the mornings when you awaken think of it as a day of endless possibility and promise. Just like a refreshing rain, so is my love and compassion for you. Let your light shine, and do not waiver in your faith. Let me handle every care and concern, for I know the best route to take and the most beneficial steps. Fear has no place in your heart today. Look to me and you will have peace in all situations, for my faithfulness never fails. Never forget…YOU are so dearly loved.

Your Heavenly Daddy

Day 6

"Your word is a lamp to my feet and a light for my path."
Psalm 119:105

Dearly Child,

Today as you walk with me, fill your mind with my truths.
Listen to words of wisdom and put them into practice;
allow them to illuminate the path before you. Believe me
when I say that I have nothing but good for you, though
sometimes it may seem just the opposite. Trust me.
Everything I do is working out a greater plan. Every hurdle
you cross is for the strengthening of your faith. Though you
cannot see the entire picture now, I am weaving a grand
tapestry in your life. With me as your guide, you and I can
maneuver the crooks in your journey, for I will surely guide
you and make firm steps for your feet. Trust Me! I am the
Way!

Your Heavenly Daddy

Day 7

"For the LORD takes delight in his people; he crowns the humble with salvation." Psalm 149:4

Dear Child,

You are my delight! I created you to fulfil my purposes here on earth. Yes, there will be times you feel afraid or inadequate, but remember *Who* you work for. I did not create you to fail but have given you the tools necessary to complete the task. Do not give doubt or fear control, for these will try and pull you away from me. Remember, the greatest of all gifts has been given to you—salvation. Put it on with all humbleness knowing that my Spirit goes with you, giving you the ability to share with others how they, too, can be my delight. I am so very proud of you!

Your Heavenly Daddy

Day 8

"Therefore I tell you, do not worry about your life, what you will eat or drink; or about your body, what you will wear. Is not life more important than food, and the body more important than clothes? Look at the birds of the air; they do not sow or reap or store away in barns, and yet your heavenly Father feeds them. Are you not much more valuable than they? Who of you by worrying can add a single hour to his life?" Matthew 6:25-27

Dear Child,

By My hand I will sustain you. Why do you worry and fret? Does it cause the difficulties to cease? Can worry still the tumultuous waters of your life? No! What it does do is to rob you of your peace. Therefore, do not worry about tomorrow; the future belongs to me. I'm already there preparing the way for you. Every step you take is orchestrated by My hand. Every provision comes from Me. I am Jehovah Jireh. I will provide. Trust me.

Your Heavenly Daddy

Day 9

"A wife of noble character who can find? She is worth far more than rubies." Proverbs 31:10

Dear Child,

You are a pearl, delicate in nature and highly valuable. I have molded you as an oyster molds a kernel of sand. Even in those moments you feel so hidden away and unimportant by the world's standards, I see you. You are unique in personality, abilities and characteristics, just as each pearl is unique in its nature. Eventually, a time will come when I will set you in a magnificent display for all the world to behold; your beauty and worth to bring glory back to myself. Never doubt or forget how highly treasured you truly are!

Your Heavenly Daddy

Day 10

"Strengthen the feeble hands, steady the knees that give way; say to those with fearful hearts, 'Be strong, do not fear;'" Isaiah 35:3-4a

Dear Child,

What is it that you're afraid of? Is it man or beast? Do you not think that I can keep you from harm? Is my arm too short to protect you in the day of trial? Have I not called you to be obedient in all things? Why then do you doubt? Why do you question *My* authority and *My* reasoning? Listen! Where I call I will supply. Trust me. Be strong and do not fear, for you do not walk alone. I am right beside you all the way.

Your Heavenly Daddy

Day 11

"If you obey my commands, you will remain in my love, just as I have obeyed my Father's commands and remain in his love." John 15:10

Dear Child,

I am honored by you. You listen and obey. My heart abounds in love for you, more than you can fathom. In times of turmoil and doubt, my truth remains. You carry that truth to those who need to hear it. Like an obedient servant you go where you are sent. Because you obey my commands, my love comes full circle and you remain tucked within its folds—wrapped like a baby in swaddling clothes. Rest there, sweet one. For it is the most perfect place to be.

Your Heavenly Daddy

Day 12

"Direct my footsteps according to your word; let no sin rule over me." Psalm 119:133

Dear Child,

Come to me with your anxious thoughts. I see the struggle within your heart as you look left and right deciding which path to take. Be still before me, sweet one. Listen to my words. Breathe in the wisdom of my love letters to you. I will show you the way. I will direct your footsteps and guide you along life's journeys, and as you trust me your faith will grow. Sin will have no place in your heart, only love for me and my will. You are so dearly loved.

Your Heavenly Daddy

Day 13

"Sow for yourselves righteousness, reap the fruit of unfailing love, and break up your unplowed ground; for it is time to seek the LORD, until he comes and showers righteousness on you." Hosea 10:12

Dear Child,

You've sat still in one place too long. It is time to rise up and do what is right. Turn over that ground of idleness and seek my will for your life. So many times you toil and spin in areas that make no impact. Today I call you to venture out and do a new thing. Allow me to work through you so that you may be a blessing to others. In doing so, you will reap a harvest of my blessing. And remember, I am right there beside you. Never doubt my power and presence.

Your Heavenly Daddy

Day 14

"You are the light of world. A city on a hill cannot be hidden…let your light shine before men, that they may see your good deeds and praise your Father in heaven."
Matthew 5:14 & 16

Dear Child,

Today is a new day…a new opportunity to shine for me. This world is darkened with sin, yet for those who have my Spirit within them, they are like a candle in a dark room; each creates a grand illumination drawing those who are stumbling and feeling their way around. Go forth and shine that light today. No one will be able to deny my presence in you. The good you do, words of encouragement you speak, deeds sewn in love, and actions taken on my behalf, will point others to me bringing that sweet aroma of praise and adoration.

Your Heavenly Daddy

Day 15

"The harvest is plentiful but the workers are few. Ask the Lord of the harvest, therefore, to send out workers into his harvest field." Matthew 9:37

Dear Child,

Do you remember back to when I first called out to you? Can you remember what it felt like to hear my voice—to feel my gentle tug at your heart? There are so many folks out there you encounter who don't know me; so many who are dying to hear my voice of hope and salvation. Yet, sadly, too many of my children are too busy with other things to point them to me. Come and ask me to raise up more willing harvest hands—those who are willing to seek out the lost and tell them the good news. Pray for yourself as well. Ask me to equip you to be a seed sewer in my vast field. I know it isn't easy. I realize it can be overwhelming and frightening sometimes but remember how much I sacrificed for you on that rugged cross. Don't miss the opportunities set before you. Go, seek, sew. Your efforts will not go unnoticed.

Your Heavenly Daddy

Day 16

"As soon as all the people saw Jesus, they were overwhelmed with wonder and ran to greet him." Mark 9:15

Dear Child,

Do you feel wonder when you think of me? Is your soul drawn to my infinite love for you, or are your feelings dulled by worldly pleasures? I have so much I want to show you; so many things I long to teach you, yet often you allow temporary things to get in the way and crowd out the wonder of who I am. Draw near me, sweet one. Prioritize your day and make time to sit at my feet in wonder and fresh abandon. As you are still in the quiet of the moment, I will breathe new life and freshness into your soul. Believe me you will be amazed by the depth of my well which knows no end. Discover the wonder in me.

Your Heavenly Daddy

Day 17

"Do not answer a fool according to his folly, or you will be like him yourself." Proverbs 26:4

Dear Child,

There are so many worldly individuals who want nothing more than to trip you up by their sinful words and actions. Do not stoop to their level. Take the high road when dealing with those who do not follow me. Let your words be loving yet seasoned with salt. Allow those around you to see a night and day difference when it comes to your reaction at the folly of others. This will not be easy. There will be times when you will be tempted to lash back, but do not do it. In those times, call unto me for help to speak only what is necessary and that which is loving. I will equip you with the strength you need in times of trial. Just ask.

Your Heavenly Daddy

Day 18

"Pride goes before destruction, a haughty spirit before a fall." Proverbs 16:18

Dear Child,

Pride is an ugly thing. I hate pride and I know full-well the damage it does to a soul. A prideful heart will do nothing more than set itself up for a perilous fall, leaving its victim to wallow in its own sludge of hurtful words, arrogant statements, and self-serving actions. Guard your heart from allowing it to become consumed with boastfulness and conceit. For when a person has a prideful heart, he or she is far from me. They have allowed self to set up his or her kingdom within the heart instead of submitting to my holy leadership and lordship. I am the only one who can successfully remove the chains of pride, but it is often a messy process. Therefore, humbly submit to me before pride latches its ugly talons into your soul. A humble heart is what I seek.

Your Heavenly Daddy

Day 19

"God is our refuge and strength, an ever-present help in trouble." Psalm 46:1

Dear Child,

When times of turmoil and storm come, run to me for refuge. I am a strong tower…a might fortress…an ever-present help. No man can thwart my plans and no power of hell can defy or steal what I have deemed to be mine. Run to me for shelter. I will cover you with my feathers like a mother hen covers her chicks. You will be safe and secure under my coverlet. I will outfit you with the most supreme weaponry and steady your feet for battle. I will give you strength to endure the storm and a peace which overcomes all darkness. Don't try to handle things on your own, sweet one. I am here ready to help. Call unto me and I will not turn a deaf ear.

Your Heavenly Daddy

Day 20

"No one can come to me unless the Father who sent me draws him, and I will raise him up at the last day." John 6:44

Dear Child,

Does a baby ask its parents to be born? Can he or she determine the day in which to make his or her appearance? Neither can a soul come into a right relationship with me unless I first woo and draw that person unto myself. So many are trying to earn or work their way into heaven by doing good works or catering to a certain religion. This is not the way. *I* am the way! Pray that those you encounter will be drawn to the Father and that the blinders will be removed from their eyes. It is my will that none should perish, yet so many turn away from me when I stand before them with arms open wide; nail prints fully visible. Point them to me, child. I desire the day in which those who are mine dine with me in my eternal kingdom.

Your Heavenly Daddy

Day 21

"Peace I leave with you; my peace I give to you. Not as the world gives do I give to you. Let not your hearts be troubled, neither let them be afraid." John 14:27

Dear Child,

Are you troubled by things of this world? Has the enemy stolen your peace and your joy? Then look to me. I am the Prince of Peace and it is my pleasure to give you peace which passes all understanding. Don't walk around feeling as if everything is crashing in around you. With me, you can overcome all of that with a heart fully at rest in me. If you will keep your eyes precisioned, focused, and your heart fastened to my truths, then I promise to fill you with so much more than what the world has to offer. Trust me. Try me. Prove me. You will see that my love for you knows no bounds. Let me show you how much!

Your Heavenly Daddy

Day 22

"Let love be genuine. Abhor what is evil; hold fast to what is good. Love one another with brotherly affection. Outdo one another in showing honor...Rejoice in hope, be patient in tribulation, be constant in prayer." Romans 12:9-10; 12

Dear Child,

When you go out into your workplace, your church, or your community, let the love you have for me shine to everyone you meet. There is so much evil out there, but evil can be overcome with good. Let love surround every word you speak—every action you take. Honor others and rejoice with them when they succeed at something, or when they receive a special blessing. By doing so, you will again display my love to them in such an extraordinary way. And when times get tough, be patient and wait for me to act. I will not leave you in the storm forever. Find things to be thankful for even in those hard times, and I will bless you and acknowledge your efforts.

Your Heavenly Daddy

Day 23

"How then will they be call on him in whom they have not believed? And how are they to believe in him of whom they have not heard? And how are they to hear without someone preaching? And how are they to preach unless they are sent? As it is written, 'How beautiful are the feet of those who preach the good news!'" Romans 10:14-15

Dear Child,

I look around and see so many who have yet to hear the good news! They do not know that I died for them. They have not heard that I am the way to eternal life. How will they hear? How will they know unless someone tells them? I am calling you today to step out of your comfort zone. I need you to be a lifeline to those who are perishing. I have placed people in your path who need to hear from you the good news of the gospel. Will you tell them? Don't be afraid. I will give you the words to say. Pray to me and you will be strengthened and given the right words at the right times. The sweetest reward will be for you to experience the fruit of your labor when that person you talked with walks into my presence. What a gift to give *and* receive!

Your Heavenly Daddy

Day 24

"For the word of the cross is folly to those who are perishing, but to us who are being saved it is the power of God." 1 Corinthians 1:18

Dear Child,

Don't be surprised by those who do not listen to you, or those who grow hostile to your committed relationship to me. They simply cannot understand. The blinders on their eyes and heart are so thick and dark, and the message of the cross to them is sheer foolishness. Yet you know that what I have said is true. You have believed in my Word…in me, and you have been saved through faith in my work on the cross. You could not have known these deep mysteries unless my Spirit revealed them to you. So, you are extremely blessed to have experienced first-hand my saving power. Lean on that power. Hold onto it with all your might. It is the difference between life and death, and it will see you through this challenging life.

Your Heavenly Daddy

Day 25

"If I speak in the tongues of men and of angels, but have not love, I am a noisy gong or a clanging cymbal." 1 Corinthians 13:1

Dear Child,

Who made the tongue? It is I who crafted it. With this one tiny muscle a person can build up or tear down. Today, choose your words wisely and carefully. It is easy to call yourself a Christ-follower, but harder to tame the tongue. Watch what you say. For if you lash out at a brother, does that build up the kingdom for good? If you tear down your husband or belittle your children, is that beneficial? No! It only creates noise—noise that harms. Instead, be one with an instructed tongue. Allow me to tame it and you will be a blessing to many.

Your Heavenly Daddy

Day 26

"But I say, walk by the Spirit, and you will not gratify the desires of the flesh." Galatians 5:16

Dear Child,

 I have given you a roadmap—my Word. It contains everything you need to know about this life and how to maneuver it. I have created it for your good, and to keep you from harmful choices. If you keep your mind clearly focused on me and apply my Words to your life, you will be able to resist those temptations by the enemy which cater to your fleshly desires. Though it may seem at times that you are being denied certain pleasures, remember that I love you more than you know and can see miles ahead of you. Trust me in knowing the best things for your life.

Your Heavenly Daddy

Day 27

"And let us not grow weary of doing good, for in due season we will reap, if we do not give up." Galatians 6:9

Dear Child,

I know the days and the to-do lists can seem endless. Don't give up! The work you are doing for me is making an impact for the Kingdom. Keep going—keep reaching out, even when it seems as if no one appreciates or even recognizes your efforts. I see what you do when it is done in secret. I know your heart and the love you have for your fellow man. There will come a time when your hard work will pay off and you will reap blessings for the help you gave. Stay the course, my sweet. I will help you persevere.

Your Heavenly Daddy

Day 28

"Now to him who is able to do far more abundantly than all that we ask or think, according to the power at work within us…" Ephesians 3:20

Dear Child,

Do you trust me? Do you know that my power and reach is limitless? Then why do you doubt? There is so much about me that you possibly cannot understand. I am not some disconnected genie, but rather the Creator God who is intricately involved in your life and can do things you cannot even imagine! Seek me and wait on my timing. I will bring things about for you when the circumstances are just where I want them to be. Keep praying. I hear you and have plans to bring you good and not harm; plans to prosper you and to give you a future. Just wait and see!

Your Heavenly Daddy

Day 29

"Indeed, I count everything as loss because of the surpassing worth of knowing Christ Jesus my Lord."
Philippians 3:8a

Dear Child,

What is the value of the possessions you have? How important are those everyday moments compared to the eternal riches I have in store for you? Nothing in this world can hold water to the relationship you have with me and I with you. I have bought you with a price. You are not your own. Even the enemy cannot come near you unless I allow it. You are precious, sweet one, and I want you to see that nothing else matters as long as you hold tight to me. Allow the fragrance of our relationship to overwhelm everyone you meet and permeate everything you do. You are chosen!

Your Heavenly Daddy

Day 30

"... Walk in a manner worthy of the calling to which you have been called, with all humility and gentleness, with patience, bearing with one another in love..." Ephesians 4:1b-2

Dear Child,

How are you different from the world? Can others automatically tell that you are mine? I have placed my seal upon your life, so you are now my ambassador in this world in which you live. Others watch you to see how you are going to act and react in different situations. Prove to them my love by walking in all humility and gentleness. Be patient and kind, not hurrying others along or trying to manipulate situations. Finally, sweet one, love like no other. This is the greatest commandment and the most fruit-bearing emotion. When we love, we demonstrate to others who we are and *WHOSE* we are. Be worthy of your calling!

Your Heavenly Daddy

Day 31

"As a father shows compassion to his children, so the LORD shows compassion to those who fear him. For he knows our frame; he remembers that we are dust." Psalm 103:13-14

Dear Child,

There are going to be many times in this life when you make the wrong choice, fail to follow, say the wrong thing, or disobey me in some way. Don't allow those times to hinder you from coming back into my presence. Though I want you to come to me and confess those things, I do not condemn you as a judge without compassion. No, I am always ready and eager to forgive and bring you back in. Remember, I created you and I know your weaknesses and the vices which often trip you up. I also know the power and strength I give you to overcome those things, so come to me and I will help you utilize the tools that you already have inside, in order that you may win the battle. I am for you!

Your Heavenly Daddy

Day 32

"Folly is bound up in the heart of a child, but the rod of discipline drives it far from him." Proverbs 22:15

Dear Child,

You know how easy it is for a youngster to find themselves in trouble? It doesn't take much prodding and the child goes his or her own way, testing the waters of boundaries set before them. So it is with you. Often you go your own way and make decisions without consulting me first. How easy it is to quickly find yourself in situations that are less than my best. So, just as a wayward child needs correction, so you, my love, need the loving discipline of your heavenly Daddy. Though I do not enjoy correcting you, I know it is best in order to teach you to go the right way and to prevent future heartache and loss. Stay firmly planted within my boundaries. This is where it is safe and full of blessing.

Your Heavenly Daddy

Day 33

"For the word of God is living and active, sharper than any two-edged sword, piercing to the division of soul and of spirit, of joints and of marrow, and discerning the thoughts and intentions of the heart." Hebrews 4:12

Dear Child,

I have given you the most important, most effective weapon of all time—my Word. This piece of armor has the ability to cut all the way to the soul, piercing the conscience of anyone who takes it up, or is on the receiving end of its message. Allow it to do its work in your heart and mind. As you get into my Word, you will read some hard truths, but I promise that none of my words will return void of doing the work I set them out to do. Because of my deep love for you, I have given you one of the most priceless gifts. Handle it with care.

Your Heavenly Daddy

Day 34

"...Let every person be quick to hear, slow to speak, slow to anger." James 1:19b

Dear Child,

I know your struggles and how hard, at times, it is for you to not lash back when someone has said something hurtful or frustrating. Pause. Think about what is being said. Is there any truth to what you have just heard? Whether it is something directed at you or someone else, always take a moment to pray about your response. I will help you sort through the emotions running through your head, and will give you wisdom about what, if anything, to say in response. Let love cover over a multitude of sins and do not give the enemy a foothold in your conversations. Shine for me!

Your Heavenly Daddy

Day 35

"From the lips of children and infants you have ordained praise because of your enemies to silence the foe and the avenger." Psalm 8:2

Dear Child,

Children simply possess a desire inside of them to praise me. There is so much joy and unconditional love in a little one. They trust without abandon, and do not question my intentions or my workings. This heart of praise causes the enemy to be silenced in their midst. This is why I say to you, "Come as a little child." Be like a little child. Have a heart so full of praise and worship, that the enemy must flee. A heart such as this is a heart that pleases me. Come sit with me awhile with a childlike heart.

Your Heavenly Daddy

Day 36

"I rise before dawn and cry for help; I have put my hope in your word. My eyes stay open through the watches of the night, that I may meditate on your promises." Psalm 119:147-148

Dear Child,

Where does your help come from? Your help comes from the Lord! I am mighty to save! When you are feeling troubled or downcast, come to me. Whether you seek me in the morning hours or in the late watch of the night, I am ready to listen and able to answer. My door is always open. I never sleep nor slumber. When you are troubled, I will fill you with peace. When you are overwhelmed, I will give you rest. When you are joy-filled, I will rejoice with you. When your grief is thicker than the outer darkness, I will comfort you and illuminate your path. You are my precious one and I love it when you come to me. Come!

Your Heavenly Daddy

Day 37

"The LORD is close to the brokenhearted and saves those who are crushed in spirit." Psalm 34:18

Dear Child,

I know that life can be so hurt-filled and difficult. Sometimes the weight of your grief or the despair from what seems like an unanswered prayer can be almost too heavy a load. Look up, sweet one! Where does your help come from? Your help comes from me. I draw near to those who are crushed in spirit. My comfort is like none other. Those who cry out of anguish of heart will seek me and find that those tears will be replaced with a deep inner peace and joy. I have such a tender heart for the hurting. Don't try to carry these burdens by yourself. Come and lay them at my feet. In my time, I will pick them up and work each of them out for your good. You must trust me and have a measure of patience. Let me help you!

Your Heavenly Daddy

Day 38

"Jabez cried out to the God of Israel, 'Oh, that you would bless me and enlarge my territory!'" 1 Chronicles 4:10

Dear Child,

I've heard your prayers. I know that you long for a larger purpose—more territory to serve in. Everything takes time. There are so many things that need to happen first, and things you must learn from the process. Take time to live in the here and now. Enjoy every moment I've created for you. Make the most of the area you've been placed in and allow me to shine through you today until the time is right for larger opportunities. Everything has its purpose and its season. Allow me to work each mundane task for the good of those who love me and are called according to my purpose. You'll see. I will do amazing things in your midst if you'll only believe.

Your Heavenly Daddy

Day 39

"Remember me for this, O my God, and do not blot out what I have so faithfully done for the house of my God and its services." Nehemiah 13:14

Dear Child,

Just as Nehemiah, my servant, sought my face during times of trial, I hear you when you come to me at those moments when everything seems as if it is stacked up against you. Don't for a second believe that I fail to see all that you do to further my kingdom. I will not forget, nor will I overlook your faithfulness. I reward those who are called by my name and who serve me with everlasting blessings. Their names are written on the palm of my hand and I long for the day that we dwell together in my heavenly place. Go forth, my child, take your rest. Your commitment to me is a fragrant offering.

Your Heavenly Daddy

Day 40

"Dear friends, since God so loved us, we also ought to love one another." 1 John 4:11

Dear Child,

Do you realize how much you are loved? Have you stopped long enough to weigh the depth of my feelings for you? I stooped down to earth in the form of my Son, and dwelt among you, then died in your place. What kind of love does that? So if you have experienced that love firsthand, then doesn't it make sense for you to offer sacrificial love to others? I know it is not always easy, but you are my hands and feet, and I desire that you love with no strings attached. Sweet one, you may be the only Jesus someone sees. Mimic Him well. For in Him I was and am well pleased, and in you also!

Your Heavenly Daddy

Day 41

"Listen to advice and accept discipline, and at the end you will be counted among the wise. Many are the plans in a person's heart, but it is the LORD's purpose that prevails."
Proverbs 19:20-21

Dear Child,

A wise person listens to sound counsel. Always make it first priority to learn and accept my Word. After that, take time to listen to others—those who are also walking daily with me and heeding my instructions. I place these people in your life for a reason. They can help you in times of decision because they know where to turn for wisdom. You can make many plans, but remember that it is my will ultimately that will prevail. Follow me, dear one. I know exactly where I am taking you. Listen and I will give you clear direction.

Your Heavenly Daddy

Day 42

"So do not throw away your confidence; it will be richly rewarded. You need to persevere so that when you have done the will of God, you will receive what he has promised." Hebrews 10:35-36

Dear Child,

Hold on to your mental strength and do not allow the enemy to plant doubt in your thoughts. If you continue to pursue after me and my will, then you will see my promises come to fruition, but be on alert, sweet one. Your enemy prowls around looking for those he can devour, and he will most assuredly attempt to side track you as you seek to follow me. Stay steadfast. Hold the line. Do not allow him to manipulate you. Cling to me and I will give you the strength and confidence you need to defeat this woeful foe. You are a warrior for me. Stand strong!

Your Heavenly Daddy

Day 43

"For we do not have a high priest who is unable to empathize with our weaknesses, but we have one who has been tempted in every way, just as we are – yet he did not sin." Hebrews 4:15

Dear Child,

Never feel as if I do not understand what you go through. I am not some lofty king who has never come down off my throne. No! I dwelt among you and felt the cold, experienced sadness, cried real tears, lamented over extreme fatigue, and walked through the lonely burden of death's door. I know exactly what you are going through and have felt the sting. Lean on me, dear one. I will carry you when it seems too much of a steep incline. Hold my hand and I will walk through this process with you. Together, we will come out on the other side of this moment and you will enjoy the glorious realization of a stronger faith and deeper understanding. Trust me.

Your Heavenly Daddy

Day 44

"In the same way, the Spirit helps us in our weakness. We do not know what we ought to pray for, but the Spirit himself intercedes for us through wordless groans."
Romans 8:26

Dear Child,

Come to me when your trials become too much to bear. Don't worry about saying the right things or saying anything at all. Speak my name and I will hear, and the Spirit who ministers on your behalf will groan in a heavenly language everything you need according to my will. That's the beauty of a relationship with me. I know you so intricately. I have every one of your hairs numbered, as well as your days. I saw you in your mother's womb and I knit you together. There is nothing about you that I don't know, therefore, I understand exactly what you need at those moments when words just won't come. Get on your knees, sweet child. I will meet you there.

Your Heavenly Daddy

Day 45

"For Christ also suffered once for sins, the righteous for the unrighteous, to bring you to God. He was put to death in the body but made alive in the Spirit." 1 Peter 3:18

Dear Child,

Have you considered my Son, Jesus? My beloved Son suffered at the hands of men according to my will, and He did this all for you! He was given over to death so that you and everyone else who believes in and accepts His death and resurrection could have eternal life with me. My Son, Jesus, did not die for those who had it all together—those who were worthy. No! He submitted Himself for those who were cast out of my presence, sinful and disobedient. That, my dear child, is true love and humility. Model that type of sacrifice for others. Give of yourself and shine for me. I promise you, it will make a difference.

Your Heavenly Daddy

Day 46

"For I am not ashamed of the gospel, because it is the power of God that brings salvation to everyone who believes: first to the Jew, then to the Gentiles." Romans 1:16

Dear Child,

When you are asked about the hope you have, what is your answer? Don't try to sugar coat it. Don't deny my power in your life. Speak up and speak boldly about the miraculous work of God. Never be ashamed or try and hide the gospel from those perishing. My Word brings life and salvation for those who put their faith and trust in its message. Everyone is invited to feast on this glorious gift. The sacrifice made was made for all. Be sure and share its saving power with grace and confidence to all who will listen.

Your Heavenly Daddy

Day 47

*"Surely God is my salvation; I will trust and not be afraid.
The Lord, the Lord himself, is my strength and my defense;
he has become my salvation."* Isaiah 12:2

Dear Child,

When times of trouble come, you can look upon me and
know that I am in your corner. Trust me to help you
through whatever you may be struggling with. You don't
have to be afraid or worry, for I will be your strength and
first line of defense. Seek my face and ask for my help. I
am not far from you and I will be your aid. Keep my words
firmly planted in your heart and allow them to soothe over
your wounds or fears, for certain they will be like a healing
balm, bringing relief and comfort. You are loved!

Your Heavenly Daddy

Day 48

"But I will sing of your strength, in the morning I will sing of your love for you are my fortress, my refuge in times of trouble." Psalm 59:16

Dear Child,

Isn't it a wonderful feeling to wake up knowing that your Heavenly Daddy cares for you? Through the watches of the night I protect you, and by day, your comings and goings never leave my viewpoint. I am your shelter. I am your place of refuge. Come, bury your burdens at the foot of my throne and I will bring answers and refreshment. Then, when that peace washes over you, I will place a new song in your heart and you will sing of my goodness and love. Listen for the notes, sweet one.

Your Heavenly Daddy

Day 49

"It is for freedom that Christ has set us free. Stand firm, then, and do not let yourselves be burdened again by a yoke of slavery." Galatians 5:1

Dear Child,

You have been set free from your chains! Why then do you go back to that former life of bondage? The evil one wants you to believe that he still has power over you. He wants you to carry the weight of your sin, but it is I, who took it off your shoulders when I was nailed to that dreadful tree. Stand firm! Don't go back down that road. You are a new creation and are created to do new things. Follow me…listen to me…learn from me. I will lead you to scale heights you never thought possible. Drop those burdens and go!

Your Heavenly Daddy

Day 50

"Therefore, as we have opportunity, let us do good to all people, especially to those who belong to the family of believers." Galatians 6:10

Dear Child,

What better way to shine for me than to do good to those around you! When the world seems dark, my light within you can be the beacon someone is searching for. Do good and you will honor me. Help others, especially fellow believers, for it leaves a fragrant aroma and promotes wholeness in the body. You are my hands and feet. By reaching out and ministering in love you demonstrate your genuine faith in me. What better testimony to a dying world! Go make a difference, my child.

Your Heavenly Daddy

Day 51

*"For this reason a man will leave his father and mother
and be united to his wife, and they will become one flesh."*
Genesis 2:24

Dear Child,

I knew from the very beginning that it was not good for
man to be alone, so I created a helpmate for him—woman.
Marriage is such a special gift. It is one of my most grand
creations as it symbolizes the commitment, love, and
intimacy of the relationship between me and my church. I
have set the husband up with the awesome task of loving,
protecting, and caring for his wife just as he would his own
body. I have called the wife to respect her husband, to love,
and to comfort him throughout the years they share
together. Today, find ways to celebrate this wonderful
treasure of marriage. Hold it close, dear one. Where two are
gathered, there I am with them also.

Your Heavenly Daddy

Day 52

"These commandments that I give you today are to be upon your hearts. Impress them on your children. Talk about them when you sit at home and when you walk along the road, when you lie down and when you get up."
Deuteronomy 6:6-7

Dear Child,

I have given you my Word so that you will have a guide map to lead the way through this journey called life. Use it wisely. Read it carefully. Remember what it says and teach others to know it as well. Live it out, don't just let the words settle in your ears. My Word is for all those who are seeking and trying to find their way. Little ones should be taught from infancy that I created them and love them. Use the knowledge that you are gaining to share with others. They will be blessed knowing that there is a God who is crazy about them too!

Your Heavenly Daddy

Day 53

"The LORD does not look at the things man looks at. Man looks at the outward appearance, but the LORD looks at the heart." 1 Samuel 16:7b

Dear Child,

You have a habit of judging a person by the outward shell—what they wear, how they look, what actions they take, but I look much deeper than that. I read the heart. I know each person so intimately. I see the *what can be* when all you see is the hopelessness. Trust me to do the work from the inside out. Pray continually for those who seem to have lost their way. No-one is a lost cause until I say they are. Today, spend time imagining what I can do with the person you have been praying for. Believe that I am working even when you cannot see. Seek out those I have appointed even if they don't meet up to your standards. Remember, I see the entire picture when you see but a reflection.

Your Heavenly Daddy

Day 54

"Better a little with the fear of the LORD than a great wealth with turmoil." Proverbs 15:16

Dear Child,

This world emphasizes material possessions. It's almost a game to them to see how many toys and trinkets each one can own. Yet I tell you that all the treasures in the world cannot compare to a relationship with me. You see, all this world can offer is empty bags—treasures that fade and rust and cause divisions. But I offer you life—eternal life that no moth or rust can destroy. Seek me. Look for me and my ways. Long for the goodness that only I can supply. In me, you will find great treasure!

Your Heavenly Daddy

Day 55

If your enemy is hungry, give him food to eat; if he is thirsty, give him water to drink. In doing this, you will heap burning coals on his head, and the LORD will reward you.
Proverbs 25:21-22

Dear Child,

What does the world tell you to do when someone has done you wrong? Get even! Repay him double! But I say, bless him! Demonstrate kindness and good deeds. When you act the opposite of what the world says or what your emotions are telling you, the results will surprise you. You will discover that the feelings of hatred you once had towards the person begin to change. You will also discover my hand of blessing as your heart is lining up with my will. Stay the course, dear one.

Your Heavenly Daddy

Day 56

A man who lacks judgment derides his neighbor, but a man of understanding holds his tongue. Proverbs 11:12

Dear Child,

You are going to run across difficult people in your lifetime—they may even live next door or work in the same office. Instead of growing aggravated or belittling them, see this as an opportunity to grow in your love and compassion. These moments you learn to hold your tongue and restrain your frustrations, you are one step closer to becoming who I am creating you to be. And who knows, but that by your actions you might win them over. Stay the course, child, and look to me for words of blessing to speak over them.

Your Heavenly Daddy

Day 57

Come to me, all you who are weary and burdened, and I will give you rest. Matthew 11:28

Dear Child,

Are you feeling tired today? I know that some days weigh heavier on you than others. Today let me help you with that load instead of trying to carry it all on your own. The burdens of this life can weigh you down, but I can take that yoke upon you and give you moments of rest. Come sit beside the still waters of my love and allow me to pour into you the strength that you long for and the peace you desire. Let me soothe you with a new song I will sing over you and revive your weary bones. I love you so!

Your Heavenly Daddy

Day 58

*...so is my word that goes out from my mouth: It will not
return to me empty, but will accomplish what I desire and
achieve the purpose for which I sent it.* Isaiah 55:11

Dear Child,

My words have power. Nothing I have spoken has been
uttered in weakness or without purpose. When you digest
my words, you are filling yourself with power and wisdom
which will not return void. For what you take in, you will
also give out. What is given out will accomplish the tasks
that I have willed it to. This is why it is crucial that you
spend time in my Word daily, and then allow your words
and actions to flow with the healing melody of my power
behind them. People will take notice. They will begin to see
my reflection in and through you. I am with you, child.

Your Heavenly Daddy

Day 59

For the message of the cross is foolishness to those who are perishing, but to us who are being saved it is the power of God. 1 Corinthians 1:18

Dear Child,

People have been tripping over the cross ever since that day my Son died for the world's sins. It is hard for them to comprehend and embrace due to their darkened minds and calloused hearts. The enemy has so fooled them into being enamored by things of the world rather than things of God. Yet you know that I am the way and the truth and the life, and that there is no other way for them to enter into a restored relationship with me. Keep your eyes clearly focused and your heart in humble reverence. You have been given a beautiful gift and the enemy cannot take it away from you.

Your Heavenly Daddy

Day 60

But when you pray, go into your room, close the door and pray to your Father, who is unseen. Then your Father, who sees what is done in secret, will reward you. Matthew 6:6

Dear Child,

You are doing a wonderful thing. Every time you go into your prayer closet and spend time with me, you are not only blessing me, but are growing in your faith. I meet you there in that secret place. I hear your heart as you pour out your concerns and your requests. I smile as the tears stream down your face while you sing a beautiful worship song to me. You are my beloved. You bring me such joy. I am there in your presence. I will never leave you nor forsake you. I will answer your prayers according to my will. I have your best interests at heart. Be still before me, sweet one. Allow my presence to overshadow any doubt, fear, or heartache. I am with you always. You are so dear to me.

Your Heavenly Daddy

If you have enjoyed these daily reminders, be sure and drop me a note. And as always, know that God loves you, is with you, and will see you through whatever you face today!

Blessings,

Kristi

www.bluelifegrind.com

www.badgeofhopeministries.com

bluelifegrind@gmail.com

29983090R00036

CINDY STEWART

AN INVITATION TO
EXPERIENCE
HEAVEN
with 49 Days of Activations

An Invitation to Experience Heaven

© 2019 Cindy Stewart

Originally published as:

7 Visions – Copyright © 2015 by Cindy Stewart.

Published in the United States of America

ISBN: 978-1-686548-72-7

Religion / Christian Life / General 15.10.01

Dedication

To the lovers of God

To all who want to know God in the deepest sense

To all who want His Word to overtake every cell in their body

To all who want to melt in His Presence

To all who awaken every day with an excitement for Him

To all who are willing to lose themselves in the obedience of His calling

To all who run the race regardless of the circumstance, knowing the faithfulness of God will see them cross the finish line

And to Him, our God, who sits on the throne, all honor and blessings to You, Father, Son, and Holy Spirit

Acknowledgments

To my sweet husband, Chay, who has encouraged me every step of the way. You are my champion and partner, always encouraging and supporting my passions. Thank you for believing in me and allowing me to run freely!

To my best friend, Karen Elisabeth Williams, who spent countless hours encountering God with me as we pressed into God's heart for this book. Thank you for all the effort in challenging every word written until it had the fullness of my heart expressed. Dreams really do come true, and you have helped me live mine!

Contents

A Note from My Personal Editor

I am not an editor by trade... I do not profess to be an expert in grammar nor punctuation nor other such knowledge. But sometimes, when editing a book for publication, it is not only about grammar and punctuation. Sometimes it is about listening, and I am a good listener.

Using the tool of listening occurs at two separate times when I am editing. The first time is when I listen to Cindy as she skillfully chooses her words to convey the message so I can help her to pull out the fullness of what God has put on her heart. Second, I listen to myself as I read and re-read the manuscript for just the right flow of words and content. Both of these practices were used to help bring about the book you hold in your hands.

One morning as I sat listening to her express what the Lord had shown her, I began to sense the Lord beckoning me to Him. And then a movie began to play mid-air; as I watched, I realized it was Heaven, and Jesus was walking toward me with a young man following close behind. A young man that looked familiar, although I knew I had never seen him before. Jesus looked at me as the young man joined Him at His side and in an instant I knew it was my grandchild that died before he was born. He was a young man now, but remained nameless, as we did not know the sex of the baby before his death. And now, I sat looking into the eyes of my grandson and my Savior. I was overwhelmed with emotion in every way.

Then there were times while working on the manuscript when God's glory would be so heavy all I could do was sit, unable to type; much less think. While other times I was so overcome with laughter my composure was completely undone as His Spirit rolled over us.

But one thing became more apparent every time I began work on this book — I would experience Jesus and the Father, some times in a familiar way and some times in a new way.

It is my desire that you too will experience Jesus and the Father and their love for you. His perfect love that makes us whole, gives us identity and purpose as we come to know more of His Heart for us and others.

A door has been opened for you to encounter the Father's love; I pray you will have the courage to step through.

Karen-Elisabeth Williams

Preface

Preparing Your Heart

These visions span a four-year time frame from 2004 to 2008; they are subject to content, and are not necessarily chronological. I knew the Lord wanted me to release them, but I did not know when or how. I have shared little snippets over the years, though never in this combination or detail.

The Lord began to prompt me to reread the visions to prepare my heart to share. It all came together when I went to my favorite encounter place, the park down the street from my house. With my sketchpad, I began to draw the gates of Heaven, and from there, God gave me the chapters and title for this book. I told the Lord I really was not a person who could take years to write a book, and if He wanted me to write another book, He had to just give it to me. He did! I couldn't do anything but write every day, and in five weeks, the writing was complete.

These visions are meant to encourage all who read them and invest in what the Lord has shared. I believe the Lord will unfold His call for you through what you will read. I also trust that you will fall deeper in love with Him.

My challenge to you is to breathe in all that He has for you by seeking Him, grabbing hold of His Word, and allowing these visions to deepen your relationship with God, moving you forward in your destiny.

Introduction

How to Get "More of God" as You Read

Where there is no clear prophetic vision,
people quickly wander astray.
But when you follow
the revelation of the Word,
Heaven's bliss fills your soul!
—Proverbs 29:18 (TPT)

Why does the Lord bring us into visions?

God speaks to us in visions that we would keep our eyes on Him. We are meant to hear God and see what He is revealing. Most visions are what I term shrouded in layers, needing to be unfolded over time that we may fully engage in what God is showing us.

15

The first time I remember having a vision, I was at my favorite park waiting on God. I was so desperate to encounter God, yet so afraid. Having been a member of a conservative church my whole life, I had never known real encounters were possible. Then I tasted the Presence of the Lord, and it stirred my hunger to get to know God, who desires to be encountered with all my being.

And so my journey has begun, and to this day, even after many encounters, my desire for the Presence of the Lord continues to blossom. I continue to be overwhelmed as He continues to pour out visions that have opened my eyes to see His heart.

The Lord has used visions in my life in several ways, which I will elaborate on in the coming chapters. However, the most frequent way was through "destiny visions." These destiny visions have led me to a path for the future. And it is through these visions that the Lord has shown me His calling on my life. Not only have these visions given me clear direction, but they are forever seared in my mind. At times, the directions have been specific and easily discerned. In other instances, the process has developed over time. *The key is to know when God has given you a vision. He is going to bring it to pass, and our job is to stay focused on Him.*

The Lord's visions have brought me into "intimacy" with Him. The weight of His glory has paralyzed me at times, but in the same breath, He holds back the heaviness so I can interact with Him. He continually teaches me to awe and fear Him as the Most Holy God, while inviting me to share in His secrets as His companion. Often it is too much to comprehend, but in the kindness of His love, I learn.

In His revealing my "identity," I was drawn into a deeper relationship. The Lord uses vision to uncover our identity. He has taught me to be His friend! He has strengthened me as a daughter, empowering me to live as an heir. As an heir, I am a warrior for Him, a healer for Him, and for Him; I release vision and destiny over others.

The Lord has used visions to "impart" and "apply" what I need in living the lifestyle He has given me to live. His impartation comes with a new ability to do things I never thought I could do. Because I am so application minded, I need to see how it works. So God often gives me the experience of practical application during the vision itself.

Through God's vision, we become aware of our wounding and failures in order to receive healing from the Lord. His visions can bring us to repen-

17

tance and forgiveness, releasing freedom from the enemy's stronghold.

I have often gained revelation, insight,and understanding about His word as well as clarity to mind-sets in our culture. These revelations have helped me release life into the hearts of others.

There is no formula to receive a vision from the Lord. He is sovereign! With that being said, there are things we can do that provoke the Lord's response. You will find keys to unlocking your eyes to see and practical exercises in encountering God, receiving visions, and journaling in *Activations 1* and *2.*

A couple of quick notes as you journey with me through these chapters: I have italicized the visions from the Lord for clarity as you read. I would encourage you to have your journal ready and allow time to encounter the Lord. He will open up your eyes to see new things.

This is my prayer for you:

Holy Spirit, my prayer for each one reading these words is that their relationship will grow deeper and their eyes will open to new visions from You. Expand their ability to see their value and destiny from Your eyes. Give them visions to write history for the King-dom and leave a legacy for the generations to come. We want our communities to fall in love with You and Your glory to be revealed on this earth.

In Jesus's Name, Amen.

1

Gates of Invitation

When God invites us into His place, He does so with purpose. He brings us in to ensure our lives will never be the same again—we are transformed by our encounter.

I stand in a vastness, void of everything, even color, until You tell me to walk forward. The vastness separates, and large gold gates appear, which I push open with ease and enter into the streets of Heaven. The gates are simple with long, thin bars. It is clean and pure and gold. I know there are bands of angels all around, but are not definable. They are more like cotton candy that flow and swirl. It is quite beautiful and soft, layer upon layers of Heavenly Host that are swirled with hues of pinks and whites. There is a celebration—it is a parade! The band is lined up on the streets of gold, and the only instrument that stands out are the cymbals banging together. And then, I am surprised to be the only one walking down the parade route, it is a parade for one—it is a parade for me!

Pause. Invite God to put you in this vision for a moment and allow Him to unfold this parade for one—you! He has commanded His gates to open wide in providing entry for you to come and join the celebration. He has set His angels swirling all around and the sound of the cymbals crashing to the rhythm of your steps. You look to see where the others are in the parade, and then delight overtakes you as the realization sets in—this parade was thrown for you! A celebration announcing the kingdom's heir has arrived!

All of Heaven knows you belong here, but more importantly, now you know! His celebration of us strengthens our identity as part of His family. The Lord will "exult over you with loud singing" (Zephaniah 3:17, ESV).

Identity Confirmed

I see in a distance a gold castle. I run as fast as I can, so fast that the things I pass are blurred, as

22

if I am driving a fast car. I arrive at the castle, and there are two guards standing by the double doors.

"Do you have an escort?" one asks. I look around and I realize I do not.

The Lord says, "I will send one."

This little angel comes up, not little as in young, but as in a small man.

He has a paper and a pen like he was checking me in.

The doors open, and the inside is rather plain and simple. Of course, I was expecting opulence. He leads me to "my room" where the inside is bare. There is a ledge protruding from the wall—stark and plain. Concrete-type walls and floor—as if a blank palate.

This? This is the room in Heaven that was prepared for me?

I sit on the ledge and look around. In the left corner opposite of me is a treasure box. The Lord has shown me this before, treasures for others. I walk over to it and lift up the lid, and beautiful treasures flow out of the box. The first thing I pick up is a beautiful strand of pearls, each pearl the size of a giant grape with gold beads between them. As I think about other things in the box, they appear.

His voice reminds me that these are His treasures for others given through me. As I encounter people and know their need, the "meeting of their need" materializes from His treasure box of Heaven.

I go back and sit on the ledge. There is a book next to me. I pick it up, and flipping through it, I notice many details of my life— it is the Book of Life. There are many empty pages since my life is not yet finished. I have this sense that this room contains all my desires. As I think I would like the room purple, it turns purple, but only temporarily. This room is being prepared for me; it is not complete as my life is not complete.

In John 14:2–3 (NCV), Jesus tells us, "There are many rooms in my Father's house; I would not tell you this if it were not true. I am going there to prepare a place for you. After I go and prepare a place for you, I will come back and take you to be with me so that you may be where I am." There are two aspects to our rooms. One is the treasures of the kingdom that have been made available for us to distribute to others. The second is our destiny on earth, splashing our walls with different hues of the events in our life.

The Lord has given us the ability as sons and daughters, heirs to the kingdom, to design our room in the Father's house. Just like in the vision, our room has access to Heaven's treasure chest. We have His treasures at our fingertips to release to others. His treasures come in different shapes, sizes, and purposes. We have freely received from the Lord, and this empowers us to freely give.

Pause. Ask the Holy Spirit, "How is my room taking shape?"

Write down what He says because it is important to record every word, picture, or direction you sense.

Treasures

The pearls are a representation of the treasure. The pearls are symbolic of what we carry. It is not a physical pearl but the representation of the pearl that is important. It is the love of Christ, which is in us. It is His love that gives us the ability to release out of us the treasures of Heaven.

These treasures are our story of how God invaded our life and our "yes to Him" reserving our room for eternity in His house. The treasures are the encouragement we have shared with others, healing we have released, wisdom we have imparted—the reality of a tangible God that lives through us. It is a reality released to other people, bringing the beauty of their room. Ask the Holy Spirit to re-mind you of all that you have released from your room and don't forget to write everything down!

Path of Completion

I am ready to go. Leaving my room, I walk to the back door. Finding myself on the other side of that door, I am surprised by the breathtaking view. There before me is a beautiful gigantic courtyard, lush with greens—so vibrant. On both sides of the courtyard is a long brick walkway that leads to an-other aspect of the castle. As I walk, I realize the courtyard is the Garden of Eden. Restored to its original beauty and purity, with trees so full, they overtakes the sky. The words to describe the detail of it escapes me. Out of the corner of my eye, it is as if I can see Adam and Eve holding hands, fully restored.

Having walked through the Garden of Eden to the other side, I realize this is the garden of resto-ration. As soon as I arrive, I look back, knowing I have to see where I have been in order to go forward. I know the castle has many, many rooms that are incomplete because the lives of the saints are not completed—for the rooms reflect their lives.

I have come to realize God has captured my heart for what He is doing by giving me glimpses of the restored— perfected—side. He has shown me I have a stake in the kingdom by completing my room through the life designed for me. My room is an invitation from the Lord to partake in the endless possibilities of releasing His treasures to others!

2

Encountering the Presence

*A*s I enter the doors, I am blinded by the glory of God. I cover my eyes and fall to the floor. I lie down—it is too much. The glory is like heat waves at the peak of summer where they can be seen in the air and felt as they roll over you. These waves of glory have no temperature. As I lie there, I am sprinkled with gold. It is thick as a fresh fallen snow all over my face and feet. I begin to crawl across the floor. I see many steps leading up to the throne. The steps have the appearance of marble as they blend into the background. There are red waves, like satin ribbons, flowing down, inviting me up. While moving closer to the throne, I can smell a sweet fragrance. I lift up my head to breathe in *more. His voice surrounds me as He speaks about the aroma of Heaven, the sweetness of the fragrance. I rise up to meet His voice. Resting my elbows on the floor, I hold my chin on my palms—I take a deeper breath.*

His wooing stirs me to move from one step to another. I struggle to pull my body forward as I am unable to lift myself to a crawl. Slowly, ascending before the King, He encourages me, waving me forward—the weight of His Presence becomes heavier and heavier—thick, though not creating resistance as I conquer the last step. I feel His Presence on me, and then suddenly, I am there—I am in His Presence. My spirit is consumed with worship. He is Holy and blessed—pure and righteous. I realize I cannot stand in His Presence though I long to stand and to see Him and to touch Him.

All of a sudden, it is as a dark, clear night, with the colors of the rainbow surrounding Him. I marvel at the colors—clear, brilliant, unspeakable colors. I know I am to stand. With help from the Heavenly Host, I rise, with my eyes fixed on Him.

My mind is saturated with the holiness of God as the words Holy, Holy, Holy resound through out me, yet I cannot utter a sound. It is beyond awesome, it is beyond spectacular, and it is beyond breathtaking.

The beauty of His Presence captures me, without fully seeing Him. There are flashes of pure white light emanating from Him and colors surrounding Him. There is movement, but my eyes are unable to discern. His hand gestures me forward, but I feel frozen in place. I am moving in my spirit, but not in my body.

The Lord woos us into tangible, authentic encounters with Him, allowing us to experience a measure of His Presence that saturates every part of our being.He permeates our cells, our minds, our spirits, and our emotions with His beauty, holiness, and wonder so we can live and breathe Him. He allows small glimpses because He wants us to be dramatically transformed into a reflection of Him.

As I am writing, I am compelled to stop because the Lord is inviting me to linger in His Presence.

Lord, You are Holy, Your sights are breathtaking, and this experience is filled with life. Holy, Holy God, rising above all others, You, God, are the only One I love.

Pause. Ask the Lord to take you into His secret place, to the encounter He has prepared for you. Read through the words slowly and pause, allowing the Lord to open your eyes to see, to fill you with the sweet fragrance of His Presence and rest under the weight of His glory. Do not miss this opportunity to experience Him. And do not forget to journal. He will expand and unfold His heart to you.

Bridal Chamber of Love

The Lord speaks. "Come, come, come and I will show you the way." We are ready to go; I stand up and shake most of the glory off me. It is fun and playful. We enter into a hallway and open up the next door.

I walk in, and ooh, the beauty cannot be described. It is the Bridegroom's Chamber. It has a canopy bed with layers and layers of sheer fabrics in different hues of purples, reds, blues, whites, creams, and pinks, with no color overpowering the other. The colors are perfectly blended.

I sit on the left side of the bed facing Jesus, and He begins to speak of love.

It is the only thing that is important.

It is what the kingdom is based on, from Genesis, "In the beginning," the creation of man, to "For God so loved the world..." It is all there is. We must learn to love through our prejudices, love through our hurts, love through our disappointments, and love through our disdain. Love and only love will prevail over all. It covers, it heals, it restores, and it saves.

I get up and walk around the room to look at all the beautiful things. The room is round, not square, representing the eternal circle. It has a settee and other furnishings, but they are not like on earth—they are familiar though not recognizable. The room is draped with the same sheer fabric that is on the bed. It has beautiful big windows to look out. And when I do, I see rolling green hills.

I go to the right side of the bed and ask if it would be okay if I lie down. It is, so I do. I am not sure if I should take a nap in the middle of the vision, but it seems right.

Jesus begins to breathe the Holy Spirit on me. He blows swirls of love throughout the room. I am soaking in love—almost as if love's fine mist of color is circling me.

I enter into what seems to be a dream or maybe a vision. I am in the field of love. I run through flowers as high as my waist. They are soft, and at times, I gather them in my arms and inhale the fragrance of love. I see to it that they never break; I am careful to respect the flowers of love. I take in their beauty as I run and laugh through the field of love. When I decide to lie down, the flowers move with me to provide a space and then cover me completely – Two created forms interacting with each other, appearing purple with yellow highlights, obscured opulence.

As I come to consciousness from the vision, I am peaceful in His presence as I lie in the Bridal Chamber. I am not sure what He is doing, but as He walks around, it is as if He is pouring into me, praying over me, breathing on me, and releasing His fullness for me. It is precious. I arise, and He is waiting—it is time to go. I have been saturated in the love of Jesus and in the glory of God.

There is so much Jesus wants us to understand about His Bridal Chamber. Where do I begin?

It is a place where we are saturated with His love. We are invited in as soon as we accept Him as our Bridegroom. Think about this for a minute.

Now, recall the life of Esther. Esther was prepared by a eunuch to become the bride of the king. For us, God our Father sent our King Himself, Jesus, to prepare us as His bride. While flooding us in His love, we become completely saturated by His love and are changed by His mere Presence. Our King has come to take out everything in us that is void of love, replacing it with a pure love—Himself.

His love washes away all our sins.

His love heals our broken hearts.

His love breaks down all barriers so we can be lovers of Him.

In the "Introduction," I shared how God gives me the opportunity to practice what I have encountered in the vision. What was impressed upon me was the open field to try out different ways Jesus imparted love. For me, I was free to run through the waist-high flowers of love. I could hold the love, smell the love, laugh in the love, and lie down and let the love overcome me. My part was to indulge and take in all the love I could, being aware of His love freely given to me.

Are you ready for His Bridal Chamber of love?

Pause. Invite Him to move you into His place and lavish His love on you. He will help you get there. You will have to give up your unbelief, hurts, and disappointments. As each hindrance is released, He will breathe into every part of you, filling it with love.

Whew! Are you ready? Are you ready? Are you ready?

HE IS!

3

Fun in the Son

Son Glasses

*A*s soon as I walk out the door, I am blinded. I cover my eyes; the light is so bright I cannot not see at all. "It is the Son," says the Father. I hear Him saying that His light shines brightly, and the closer you are to the Son, the brighter it shines. As the Son shines down on earth, the beams are met with many filters — filters of filth, sin, unbelief, and warfare. His light becomes dim and hardly recognizable. As My people draw closer to the Son, His light will illuminate within them until they reach Heaven where they are able to stand with the Son shining in His fullness. A pair of "Son" glasses are handed to me from the Father, which allow me to approach the

Son. I glance over at the Father and giggle; God knows my love of humor. At this point I feel as if the glasses are not protecting me as much as they are protecting Him from my less-than-resurrected body. His light is not Him, it emanates from Him, and as I come closer, I am able to hug the light. It is not without form. It is warm and bright and rubs off on me. As I put my arms around the middle of His light and rest my head against Him, He actually responds in kind. His waist is formed for me to hold, and His chest is soft for me to rest. It is forever, but not long enough. Then I know it is time to go.

Jesus is God, *He is Holy*, He is to be feared and worshiped—all this is true. But then, there comes a revelation in the awareness of God that is greater than the understanding we have. He gives us illumination of a fuller understanding in our encountering Him. For me, the Father's word play of the "Son" glasses was for my benefit. It was a bridge for me, because it was something I could relate to allowing me to move closer to the bright holiness of Christ. The glasses helped to shift my expectation of what I thought it would be like to encounter Jesus in His Majesty, in His Holiness, in His Glory. Once I had put the glasses on, I was able to approach Him and lean fully in, becoming immersed into Him. I was the one who had changed. And so God in all His goodness, in all His kindness, and out of His plan allows us to touch Him, see Him, and encounter Him in His holiness. It is juxtapose, a strange tension between the weight of His holiness gluing us to the floor unable to move and His mercy permitting us to rest our head upon Him. We must be careful not to make doctrine hold to "God is Holy" or "God is touchable." It will never be one way or the other—*He is Holy and He is touchable.*

God surprises us in moments when we think we have Him all figured out by expanding our minds. We are looking for the concrete when God is infinite and eternal.

God is Holy and to be feared and worshiped—touchable and visible, while providing us a place to rest.

Allow God to bring you to the experiential revelation of both sides to experience His holiness, be overwhelmed in His Presence and have a stuck-to-the-floor encounter.

And experience Him in the tenderness and warmth of His embrace.

Be sure to capture these moments with Him. Write, draw, using color and images as a reminder to the truth He unveils.

Tour of Heaven

Leaving the presence of Jesus, continuing on the brick walkway, I round the corner and become aware I have lost the Son glasses. After stepping onto the overlook, leaning forward on the half wall, I am captured by what I see.

At first there are layers and layers of puffy clouds, and then the clouds separate like curtains at a theater, and it is a spectacular sight. It is a panoramic view of all that is pleasing to God.

To my left are the heavens. Stars upon stars, planets, universes, the heavenlies—all are dramatic: magnificent, beautiful, and shiny!

I love the sky and how it illuminates the night. As I scan the heavenly view, my eyes catch a glimpse of the Heavenly Host. Like watercolors, I know they are there, I know their shape, yet I am unable to convey this verbally. A daunting host arrayed in a Thor-like helmet with pointy shoulder wings stand out in the midst of my view. Creatures among creatures...layers upon layers. I know who they are. It is the life of Heaven unfolding before my eyes. At the same moment, I watch the ever-changing motion of His Heavenly Host. With His Presence standing beside me, He permeates the atmosphere, hovering over it and saturating the very creation, because He is God!

I have had such revelation of the Oneness, the Oneness of the moment to moment...the interchangeability of the Oneness...the Oneness between the Father, Son, and Holy Spirit. It is the Oneness of God I encounter—the Lord. I am blinded by the glory of God, and at the same time as I am blinded by His glory, I approach the King—Jesus. While in His Bridal Chamber with Jesus, He breathes His most intimate breath on me—His Holy Spirit. In a seamless exchange, the Father ushers me in to see the brilliance of His Son as He, the Father, translates me through the brilliance of His Son to the majestic view of Heaven's extent.

Although, They (Father, Son, and Holy Spirit) are the very essence of fluidity and seamlessness, They are not without physicality.

The Oneness Is the Dynamic Interaction of the *Trinity* without Walls!

Jesus has my hand and is walking me around. He opens the doors, showing me the different rooms.

The first room is the Lightning room, where all the lightning is stored for the throne room.

The next room is the Righteousness room. Jesus opens the door, and it is bright white, almost blinding.

Then Jesus and I are standing in the Council room of the Lord. It has a circular table of dark wood with the center cut out. It is really beautiful. It looks like it could be an information desk. There are men sitting at the table in the center facing out. They all look exactly the same. At first I see only angels, but when I sit down, it is the Father who sits across from me. I begin to tell Him everything on my heart. As I sit face-to-face with the Father, there is such tenderness and permission to just be transparent. I rest my head on the table while I talk to Him.

A moment passes, I open one of the doors, and it is the Room of Knowledge. I take the large red buttons like a clown would wear, each labeled with Word of Knowledge or Knowledge of the Lord. As I pick them up and pin them on my shirt, I feel this great affection from Jesus, a joy and laughter from being with me with a tenderness toward my naivety.

He says, "You do not need to wear these buttons. You have access to it all."

I look at the next door, and it is open. I see musical instruments that represent "instruments of worship."

We take a few more steps to the next room, which contains blueprints, tools, compasses, walking sticks, rolls and rolls of plans and instructions—all that I would desire to know is in there.

I go around the door to the room with body parts. Standing in the threshold of the room seeing the body parts, He speaks to me without words, reminding me of my prayer for someone's knee to be healed the night before. And then, He voices, "You do not always need to ask for healing and repair. You can ask for a new one. I have shown you this room before." I instantly recall the testimony of a lady who required a knee replacement, and the person who was praying for her just reached up to Heaven and grabbed a new knee, replacing the old. Her knee was made new. I walk by the Miracles and Wonders door and hesitate. And He says, "That is yours too, treasures, prosperity, they are all yours. This is your house. You have complete access."

I cannot say I understood all He was showing me, but I just know there was an "aha" moment. The simplicity of the doors is Him showing me the access I have to the things I have hungered after.

I read the book *Momentum* by Eric Johnson and Bill Johnson.They were writing in the context of spiritual inheritance: "Spiritual inheritance pulls back the curtain and reveals what we already have permission to possess."

The doors (curtains) of my spiritual inheritance have been opened, giving me permission to release what I possess.

What has God given you permission to possess?

For years, God has given me presents on my birthday and on Christmas Eve. In 2012, He gave me a "stamp of approval." God has opened the doors and stamped the usage of these things "approved," because it is part of our spiritual inheritance.

What has He stamped Approved for you?

Don't skip this step. With every minute you spend talking with Him about these things, there will be more curtains pulled back, doors opened, and promises, plans, and purposes stamped—APPROVED!

4

Touch of Freedom

*W*e start down a hallway to the entrance of a spiral staircase, which leads into the dark and musty room. I am shocked at what I see. There are people chained to the wall—it is a dungeon. They are all but skeletons with very little left of them, flesh but no substance clinging to life, dangling by chains as in a scary movie.

"What is this? How can this be in Heaven, Lord?"

The Lord answers, "This is a mirror of what is happening on earth. My people are in chains."

I go over to them, and as I touch them, the chains fall off and color rushes back into their faces. Their normal features restore as they come back to life. They are smiling and laughing. We are all hugging *and kissing as Jesus watches. That was all it took, a touch in the Presence of our Savior, and they are set free.*

I turn to Jesus, and with a nod of His head, I know it is time to go. I say good-bye.

This is what Jesus wants us to know; all we have to do is extend our hand. Freedom! Jesus purchased freedom from all types of oppression, bondage, and sickness. Through this vision, He showed me how it only takes one touch. Our touch frees people from the bondage—the chains—that restrains them from their destiny and the abundant life Christ purchased.

When Jesus sent His disciples out, He gave them power and authority to "heal the sick, raise the dead, cleanse those who have leprosy, drive out demons. Freely you have received; freely give" (Matthew 10:8, NIV). What was even more interesting, Jesus sent them out in teams without Him. For months, they traveled the region doing exactly what Jesus empowered them to do—"touching" the people they encountered. They returned excited to tell Jesus of those who were in chains that had been set free. The disciples had moved in power and authority, releasing freedom, just as Jesus showed them to do.

We are the disciples of Jesus!

We have been given the power and authority of the Holy Spirit to break all types of oppression, bondages, and sickness. When we have experienced the power of Jesus in our lives, we can freely give what we have freely received from Him.

Remember His promise to us:

I tell you this timeless truth: The person who follows Me in faith, believing in Me, will do the same mighty miracles that I do—and even greater miracles than these, because I go to be with My Father! For I will do whatever you ask Me to do when you ask Me in My name. That is how the Son will show what the Father is really like and bring glory to Him. Ask Me anything in My name and I will do it for you! (John 14:12–14, TPT)

Do you want to be in the "freedom business" doing the same "mighty miracles" that Jesus did?

Read this declaration aloud over yourself:

Lord, I want to set people free and move in power and authority.

I declare I believe Your Word.

I declare Your Holy Spirit lives in me.

I declare I have Your power and authority.

I declare healing for the sick and freedom for the oppressed.

I declare I am obedient, following Your lead. Thank You, Jesus!

I just want to tell you a little bit of about my passion for healing—I want everyone healed!

When I started out, I studied Scriptures, read books on healing, and received great impartation. Many years ago, my friend and I started a healing ministry. We were a hungry team who faithfully studied, worshiped, and practiced together. Since then, we have opened Healing and Encounter Rooms to bring freedom to our community.

Through our teaching, with impartation, and activation others have been released to bring freedom in their homes, offices, neighborhood, and even at the grocery store. I want to encourage you to find people who burn with the same passion for freedom. Find those who want to grow, learn, and practice setting people free. God needs people who want to release His freedom.

5

History Writer
Identity and Destiny

*B*ack up the stairs and out on the other side of the castle...

Jesus now shows me a nondescript object in His left hand. It is not round or square, but it is soft yet firm.

It has a hue of red, but it is not red.

I do not understand what He is showing me, yet I desire it to be discernible.

This form in His hand is nondescript. It is something I know by my spirit, but my mind cannot grasp. I look to Him for the answer, and He shows me a world that has no description—it is empty.

It does not become descriptive unless there are people. The object in His hand is the world, formless until He filled the world with us—His people, His DNA, His character, and His essence. He shows me that He made us perfect; it is the sin that creates the imperfection.

He wants me to see that even with the imperfection, the world is nondescript without us, and He designed us to give the world description. We are the "describers," His signature on the world. We must allow Him to write our story and to make our mark as history makers in this finite time. Each of us has our own defined place in history, and it cannot be minimized. No one can be in this world without leaving his or her mark.

Do you realize that everything you do leaves your mark in history for the Kingdom of God? Our personal footprint is cemented forever in our season of life on this earth, and our footprint leaves a positive impact or a negative impact. One of the greatest needs in the Christian life is to understand our identity and our destiny. I work with people on a regular basis who do not realize either. It is our calling to assist one another in the discovery of what God has designed in creating each one's personal footprint.

There are several common core inhibitors to our personal footprint that keep us from our identity and destiny, though not inclusive, but areas I see regularly. Each one of these areas are redeemable in the eyes of God. They are woundings from family of origin, life of sin, and church brokenness.

Wounding from Family of Origin

Interestingly,I have worked with people whohave come from a healthy family, but have deep wounding which hold them back, and I have worked with those from a dysfunctional family who are virtually unscathed. My point being, it is not always the type of family that creates the captivity. It can be the vulnerability of your soul that creates a barrier that keeps you from moving forward. In my experience, I have seen the Lord reveal how one word spoken to a child can bring fear for years to come. Once the revelation of the origin of the lie is revealed, you are able to renounce the lie of the enemy, hear the truth from God, and be set free. The goal is to ask the Lord to reveal any hidden lies holding you back. It is possible that you might need assistance in this process, which is available through inner healing ministries such as Sozo with Bethel Church, Redding, California; Christian Healing Ministries, Jacksonville, Florida; and our

Healing and Encounter Rooms at the gathering with Jesus, Tarpon Springs, Florida, just to name a few.

Ask the Lord if there is an area of bondage resulting from your family line.

If you sense a "yes" from Him, then ask Him to direct you to the path of freedom.

Life of Sin

We make mistakes in our lives, some more crippling to our future than others. I have found one of the greatest challenges is recognizing our sin and then applying the finished work of Jesus Christ to set us free from the sin.

The finished work of Jesus being, He forgives you and remembers your sin no more—not because He has a bad memory. No! The blood of Jesus shed on the cross washes away every sin you have committed, leaving you free from guilt and shame. The shackles that have held you back from being everything that God created you to be are now gone! Jesus does not want us to live in bondage to our past; He wants us to be set free for our future.

Our challenge is to ask for forgiveness and then receive and believe Jesus for the clean slate He has purchased for us.

52

Do you need freedom from your past?

Is there an area you need to receive God's forgiveness? Do you believe He wants you to be set free?

Go to Jesus now, lay it all on the table before Him, and allow Him to take your sin and wash you clean.

Church Brokenness

The church family should be the safest place in the world; however, that is not always the case.

Why? It is because we are broken people who have not allowed the grace and the mercy of Jesus to overtake our lives and transform us.

In one of the visions, the Lord let me look through the *Book of Life*, I was so overjoyed in seeing the names of those already in Heaven and names of others who were still living.

Then He gave me another book...

I am sitting on the marble steps in the Throne Room, and Jesus places another book on my lap.

It is massive—huge and heavy. It has a dark-brown leather cover with string binding. The edges of the linen-like pages have frayed from the passing of time. With the antiquity comes a layer of dust with a musty odor as I open the cover.

Looking at Jesus, I ask, "What is this, Lord?"

"These are all the people I am drawing to Me." I am amazed.

Jesus continues, "These are the people the church pushes away from Me. I draw them in, and you push them back out."

Sobering... Heartbreaking...

I really do not know how to respond because I know this is true. I know I have been a part of pushing people out.

Jesus elaborates, "The Church has set up so many boundaries that it is very difficult for My people to get in. Fight for Truth and Protect My People. Fight for Truth and Protect My People."

His voice echoes. "Fight for truth and protect My people." As it reverberates, it becomes an impartation, a mantle, a mandate burning within me.

Please do not misunderstand what is being said here. The Lord wants a bride who is healthy, fair, and lovely. He has laid the plans out clearly to accomplish His desires. It is we, the body, who are struggling to meet this goal.

Because we struggle with our identity and with our destiny as His body, the ones who do not know Him yet are held at bay.

The biggest challenge I have encountered is the lack of value and honor we extend to one another regardless of position—we all bear responsibility. We tend to see what is wrong instead of looking through the eyes of God and seeing their true identity and destiny. It is a continuous battle for us with each individual life that crosses our path. Not all who enter in will be ready to be transformed.

6

Unzipped

Father," I call, "Father..." " Yes, child," He answers.

"Where am I?"

"You are on the streets of Heaven," He replies.

"Why?"

"This is where you desire to be, so I have brought you here," He says.

"It is so beautiful, Lord. Show me, Lord, what is on Your heart. Show me what You long for me to see," I plead.

It is like a zipper opening up where I can see the earth. Puffy clouds pass by my view. I peer down to a scene of skyscrapers, bumper-to-bumper traffic in both directions that is slowly moving through *the streets, and bustling people dressed in coats and hats.*

"What is on My heart is not here (Heaven). It is down there. My heart is beating for My people. It longs for all to know Me. I want to heal their broken hearts. I want them to know Me— really know Me."

We zoom in on a girl with a fuzzy creamy-white hat. She appears to be in her early thirties, with wavy shoulder-length blond hair, and wearing a camel coat.

"These are the ones who think they know Me, but they do not. They only know about Me, and they do what they have been taught." I know exactly what He means as He speaks. Culturally relevant, dressed in high style, she is uptown posh, bound by knowledge without intimacy with the Lord.

The view now zooms in on a man who is walking with a Wall Street swagger, displaying autonomy. Dark hair, dark clothes, nicely dressed in a wool coat.

"Then there are those who deny Me though they know better," He continues.

Like the man, lost in his day, never looking up, they walk in this defined purpose of where they are going, doing what they please, pushing God's beckoning aside.

After that, we zoom in on a row of homeless people gathered in an alley, sitting in a line on the cold road, leaning against a red brick building. There is one whose face we can see is smudged with dirt and hair matted. His filthiness masks who he is. But his eyes though dark and hollow still have a shimmer of light.

God continues, "Then there are the homeless, the broken, and rejected ones—the ones that cannot cope with life itself. That is what is on My heart— My people who are called by My Name."

In all, there is a physical allocation in representing the world, but that allocation is empty without the inclusion of the Presence of God. The problem isn't being successful or affluent or homeless, the problem is operating without the Presence of God fused into these lives. Without the Presence of God in our lives,we are lost and without purpose.

I inquire, "What do we do, Lord?"

"Pray to Me, and I will show you how to reach My people. I will send every heart that is available to Me to help My people. It is the one heart that makes a difference in My kingdom."

Pray to Me

For years, I start my morning with the same question: "What is on Your heart, Lord?"

His heart is for the people He created in His image to join His family. Every person born has an innate desire to know and to worship the Lord. He needs each one of us to see with His eyes into the hearts of others. The Lord is asking us to pray to Him, and He will show us how to reach them.

Stop: Think about the people you know who fit these descriptions:

1) Ones who think they know the Lord but only have knowledge of Him

2) Ones who do know the Lord but choose to live independent of Him

3) Ones who are broken and rejected— paralyzed by their circumstance

Tell the Lord your heart is available to make a difference in these lives. Write their names down, pray for them, and listen for God's instructions. Be ready to reach each person!

Zipped Closed

Then the opening zips close, and I am on the streets of Heaven again. "Continue on," He says, "this is where all My people come and enjoy the celebration of Heaven, to walk the streets of gold, to hear the sound of Heaven, and to be a part of the Heavenly Host. Such is My desire.

"I draw them, and My true disciples on the earth encourage them. They provide understanding, a safe place for them to learn about Me, experience Me, and love Me. We are in this together. I chose from the beginning of time to include My children in My place, and I have. This is how it has been done from the beginning. I sent My Son to train disciples and to leave a blueprint for the future generations to follow. We will prevail," He proclaims.

"Father, as I write 'We will prevail,' I want to write 'We have prevailed' because the victory has already been won through the Cross and the Resurrection," I say out loud.

"Yes, this is true, but My disciples on earth, like you, must prevail each day in My Name to accomplish the plan set before you," He clarifies.

"Lord, I know my mind is so simple sometimes. Forgive me. My question is, how are we doing?"

Laughter, soft and gentle, billows over me from the throne. "Some days good, some days not so good. This is life here on earth. There are ups and downs, enemy strongholds and releases. We are always in a battle for My people, My Church, and My Word. The end has been won, but the battles are many."

You are part of Abba's beautiful plan to increase the population in Heaven! He has designed you as an encouragement to others, providing them a safe place to learn and grow in the Presence of the Lord. He knows we go through seasons of great victories and seasons of great struggles. Nevertheless, while we are in our earthly bodies, there will be ongoing battle for the people of God. He has given us the blueprints and strategies to defeat the enemy and have victory over each heart.

Don't let this revelation pass you by. Declare it now:

"I am part of Abba's beautiful plan to increase the population in Heaven! He has designed me as an encourager to others, providing them a safe place to learn and grow in the Presence of the Lord."

Glory

"There will be a release of revival through the land, pockets of My glory to the faithful that will draw those I have shown you. There will be a renewal of relationship with Me for those who have walked away, and healing will rain down like a

flood. Be expectant and be accepting of who is placed before you. This will not be limited to the church building—this will happen in your grocery stores, on your streets, in your parks, at your schools. Do not be afraid. Have faith."

The Lord's release of revival and His glory bring a picture of fireworks lighting up a dark sky to my mind, a celebration. As citizens of Heaven, we are to celebrate what God is promising—revival, glory, relationships renewed, and healing raining down like floodwaters.

As I write, I know this promise is being fulfilled. We are seeing hearts turned back to the Lord and a new hunger for Him. Healing is becoming more of a reality, not just in our churches but as we go in our day-to-day lives. God is faithful to His Word and to His people. His words become like motion censors when they are spoken, causing all creations on earth and in Heaven to be activated to respond.

7

Go! Go! Go!

*O*ut in the distance, I can see what seems to be a
horizon—an endless ocean with the perfect reflection from the sun shining on it. "This is all mine,"
He says, "and I give it to you. The vastness and the
beauty, the fullness of life and joy and laughter—it
is yours. All I have I give to you. Use it wisely. Take
care of this gift. Steward these things with My heart
and My character. I love the vastness, I love the fullness of life, and I love My people. Take care of them.
The world was created for completeness, and it will
be complete. Until that completion, take care of My
world. Be a good steward of what I give you. I trust
you."

"Thank You, Lord, I will, though I cannot do it without You." I smile.

"You have Me. I am with you. I will guide you in all things. Seek Me and listen for My instructions. I am with you."

"This seems daunting, Lord. How? What?"

"I will guide you. You will be responsible for what I intend, and I will show you clearly. You will not have to guess. Open your mind to the vastness before you. Move out of the limited thought you have. This is why I have shown you this. Drink in the vastness of life. Enjoy the vastness of possibilities and opportunities to serve My Kingdom. Join in! There is much we will accomplish together by My Spirit to glorify My Father. JUMP IN, CINDY."

There are "basic responsibilities" the Lord has given us, which are clearly revealed in Scripture. These "basics" are to flow out of us as naturally as breathing, like honor, love, kindness, sowing and reaping, and caring for the land and all of creation. We become more proficient in these basics as we grow in our love for the Lord because our heart becomes like His. We know what His heart loves, so our heart loves the same, and we know what breaks His heart, so we know what should breaks ours.

Stop: Ponder this over the next few days and ask the Lord to heighten your sensitivity to His heart. Ask Him to grow your love for His heart and increase your proficiency in these basics responsibilities. Journal what He shows you and how it is affecting others.

Jump In, Cindy

We are now standing on the end of a platform at the castle when Jesus says to jump, and now He is helping me step up on a ledge. I look over my shoulder, and I am met with a smile and a nod.

I wait because I'm thinking we will jump together. Suddenly, I realize I have to jump first.

So without hesitation, I jump.

I float freely down through the sky and the clouds, filled with wonder and laughter. I look to my right, and there He is—beside me.

"You needed to jump alone, but you are never alone. When you said 'yes' and jumped, you jumped to all that I have. Thank you."

It is strange to hear Him thank me. I do not know how to reply.

"Are you ready?" He asks. " Yes," I reply.

As we float through the air, my attention shifts to the city below.

It is like a movie, floating like Mary Poppins without the umbrella.

We land in a beautifully landscaped park. Trying to figure out where I've landed, at first I think it is Central Park but change my mind, thinking I am in Paris. There is a large multi-tier pedestal stone fountain with water flowing from the top.

As we stand next to the fountain, Jesus begins to speak. "I am the living water flowing from the top. I am the healing river that rushes under your feet. I am the beauty inside of you that shines for others. I AM!"

We walk through the park, enjoying the beauty in silence. Then out of the park into the streets, like New York City, but not. No noise, no manic behavior—no hurried bustle of crowded streets. It is as if time is standing still. There are cars but no movement. We are the only ones in motion. A lady with long blond hair and a dark, navy wool coat, head slightly turned with groceries in her arms, halts by the Presence of Jesus; she becomes highlighted to me.

"We are here," He says. "What is all this?"

"This is the earth and all that is in it. This is your proving ground to cultivate all that I have

68

given you, like the talents. I am releasing you to all the earth. Go forth and make disciples for Me. Multiply My Kingdom on earth as it is in Heaven. Release Me to all you encounter. GO! GO! GO!"

"You like threes," I say with a smile in my eyes as I glance at Him.

"I am with you. Do not be afraid. Do not be terrified. I am the Lord, your God, and I am with you. Nothing will be too hard for you, for I am with you. Seek Me, ask Me, and I will answer you and I will protect you. Dig in, we have much work to do. Remember, enjoy what you do; no matter how difficult it may seem, there will be victory. I am with you. Have faith and believe, and you will find joy in every circumstance. I am with you. I love you. You are Mine."

"Good-bye, I must leave you in My physical state, but I will always be with you in the Spirit. Remember these words, share them with others: I love you. I love you."

Then He is gone.

My lips are saying I love You too, as I stand in the middle of the city with cars and people around me still motionless. I say, "Go," as if I lack the faith to believe they would move. So I say it again. Only this time with more confidence, and EVERYTHING begins to slowly move. I doubt that it is really happening, and with my doubt, everything slows down. The outside reacts to my inside as God shows me the power of believing. When I'm choosing to believe, everything begins to move.

Then, His voice rolls over me firmly as His words press into me. "All authority and power of Heaven and Earth have been given to you. Speak on My behalf, act on My behalf, and heal My people. I love you."

I continue walking through the city. It is still quiet, or maybe I just cannot hear the noise. I am thinking and contemplating His words, so many words. "Go" is anchored in my mind.

I walk on. Arriving at the subway entrance, I sit on a bench. As people pass by, they first stop in front of me. Frozen in time, I look inside of them. I have x-ray vision into their hearts. I am seeing their hearts broken, the very thing that is holding them back. Suddenly, I get up and go down into the subway and step into a car. As it begins to move, I stand and say, "Jesus Christ lived for us, Jesus Christ died for us, and Jesus Christ rose from the dead and sits at the Father's right hand! How many of you need a healing today? In Jesus's Name, be healed!" And they are All Healed!

I continue, "How many of you want to know Jesus?" And I pray a prayer of salvation with them.

Unexpectedly, I appear in a classroom at a college lecture hall. The hall is enormous, with rows and rows in the amphitheater-like setting. There is no transition—in the blink of an eye—I begin the same process with the room full of students. They are captivated by what I am saying. It is their appointed time to hear the basics, to receive healing, and to be invited into a life with Christ. Their hearts have been prepared to receive, it has become their "Go" moment.

Are you ready to *jump* into all Jesus has for you?

Join me in the journey of bringing His reality into yours.

This is the prayer I prayed in the vision.

I will go, Lord. I will receive all You have for me. Stretch my mind to a bigger understanding. Expand my ability to comprehend. Jesus, Savior, thank You for giving me this beautiful gift, thank You for trusting me, and thank You for loving me. In Jesus's precious Name, Your Name is above all names, I bow down to You. Yes, I will go. I love You. Amen.

Activation 1

Going after Visions

Going after visions is really going after God! God wants us to pursue Him, draw close to Him, and spend time alone in His Presence.

The key to going after God is deciding it is going to be a journey of eternity with Him. When we invest in reading His Word, talking to Him, worshiping Him, spending time with Him, and listening to Him, it changes who we are. God never changes; it is us that need to be transformed into His likeness. As we are changed, then we actually begin to see God for who He really is, not who we want Him to be. With this comes freedom to be who He created us to be!

Let's get started!

The Word is intentional. If you will be intentional about walking through these next 7 weeks with God, your life will be wrecked! You will soar to new heights in love and in the Presence of God.

Five Steps to Encounter

1) Welcoming God

The Lord is always with us, so the first thing we do is to acknowledge His Presence. When I wake in the morning, I take time to talk with Him about what is on my mind. I thank Him for all that He has done and what He has planned for the day. I always ask Him what is on His heart. God is interested in us, and yes, He knows all things. However, He has designed us for a real, tangible, interactive love relationship.

2) Worshiping God

Worship is expressed in different ways; nevertheless, the foundation of worship is our love and affection focused on exalting God for who He is and what He has done. Personally, because I love music, I use it as my springboard to launch my worship. There are also times where I will read Scripture out loud, worshiping God with His own words or write my worship to Him in my journal.

At other times, I draw, walk through the park while worshiping Him for all He has created, and even dance! God created us uniquely in the way we express worship. It can flow out of us in all types of formats, depending on the season we are in. In the 7-week journey, we will engage in a variety of ways to express our worship to the Lord.

3) Meditating on the Word

The Word of God is His breath blowing trans-formation into our lives. It is our lifeline and blue-print. The Word lives and breathes life into us each time we read it. It also opens us up to the Pres-ence of God, revealing His nature, His character, and His design for us. His Word is vast and far-reaching while personal and intimate. Reading and meditating on His Word are critical in our ability to encounter Him, hear Him, and know His will. While you are meditating, the Lord may impress on you to read the entire chapter or a few verses before and after. Be steadfast in following His lead. Allow Him to deposit seeds of understanding that will grow and develop as you go.

4) Listening for Him

Hearing from the Lord in this busy world takes training. Quieting ourselves and allowing the sound of His voice to come through are acquired endeavors. There are several keys to increasing our receptivity in hearing Him.

One key is being open to the Lord communicating in a multitude of ways: through His Word, fragrances, sounds, numbers, colors, dreams, pictures, and other people. We learn the rhythm of His interaction by our time spent with Him. Recently, the Lord gave me a prophetic word for the coming year. He spoke to me in five dreams, as well as awakening me to the consecutive numbers 3:33 and 4:44 on the display of my digital clock. Another key is not letting the distractions overtake you. I keep a notepad near me, so if things I need to remember come into my thoughts, I write them down and release them. If there continues to be an interruption, I will read the Scripture out loud or repeat Jesus softly until peace is released. Over time, I have learned to recognize the Lord's communication, and then I ask Him, "What are You saying to me?" And I wait as His message unfolds.

5) Journaling

Recording your daily encounters with the Lord is critical. There are so many times the Lord is speaking to us, and it is over time we recognize His voice and what He has been saying. Journaling captures the details of the moment, securing your feelings, your thoughts, and what God is showing you. So over time, when looking back, it allows us to separate our emotions, our beliefs, and what He has said, revealing His movement in our life. The other important aspect is keeping His promises to you in the forefront so you stay on the path He has for you. There are many promises the Lord has given me that have come to pass, like writing and publishing books. But there are still promises I am waiting for, and I keep them in front of God, talking to Him about them and declaring them over my life. Knowing that God is faithful to what He has promised, He will fulfill all that He has spoken to us!

Here is a sample of how each day unfolds as you follow the five steps to encounter in the 7-week journey found in Activation 2.

Sample: Each day, there will be a Scripture listed for you to apply the steps. I encourage you to look up the Scripture in your Bible so you are prepared for the Lord to lead you through other passages.

Week One, Day One

"Because I live, you will live, too. I am in the Father and you are in me and I am in you" (John 14:19–20, NCV).

Welcoming God: Lord, I invite You as the One who lives in me to open me to all You desire to show me in this passage. Thank You for being with me and giving me Your Word to follow. Thank You, Jesus, for living in me and making me one with the Father. Lord, what is on Your heart for me today? My desire is to encounter You and have a tangible touch from You. Thank You, Lord.

Worshiping God: Lord, I worship You as my Savior. Thank You for living in me and opening the way for me to know the Father. Lord, I look to You in all things, and I honor and praise You. Abba, I worship You for Your Father's heart and deep love. I praise You for our time together and this incredible opportunity to hear Your voice. All honor to You, Holy God!

Meditating on the Word: Lord, I will meditate on John 14:19–20 until I sense You move in my spirit. Connect me to Your heart for this Word.

Listening for Him: Speak to me, Lord. I am listening for You.

Journaling: Lord, as I meditated on this verse, I saw these stackable Russian dolls. When I took the top off, there was another inside, and another, and another. Abba, I see Your chest opened, and I see Jesus entering in Your heart and then me into

Jesus's heart. Then I see my chest open, and both of You enter into my heart. Always together, we are all one. Sear this truth, Lord, like a branding iron within me, so as I go today, I will not forget who I am carrying. I love You. Thank You, Amen.

Enjoy your time with Him in the 7-week journey.

Activation 2

7-Week Journey

Forty-Nine Days of Encounter

Welcome to the 7-week journey!

I asked the Lord what He wanted to say to encourage you as we spend the next forty-nine days wrapped in His presence. This is what I heard:

"Thank you for desiring to spend time with Me. I am overjoyed with your hunger. Each day, I will come to you in ways which will grow us closer together. I will expand your ability to understand as we work together. My arms are wide open, and My heart readied to pour over you. Be encouraged by our time together. My love is for you."

Each day, read the Scripture(s), and using the format described in Activation 1 (*Welcome God, Worship God, Meditate on His Word, Listen to Him, and Journal*), allow God to breathe on you and open you up for an encounter. Have fun and enjoy this life-changing adventure with the Lord.

Lord, over these forty-nine days, release Your Presence with those seeking You. Protect them and order their day, filling it with You. Give them dreams and visions of You. I bless You and honor You, dear Lord.

Thank You for Your yes to this request. In Jesus's Name, Amen!

Let the encounters begin!

Week One

There is an excitement in this and expectation to come. Stop and take a deep breath. God has incredible things planned for you. Don't put too much pressure on yourselves!

Allow God to guide you through each day—He has a plan. Remember, He may want to rid you of things that have held you back, and if that happens, do not allow any condemnation to overtake you.

Abba is your Father who you can trust and who provides His very best for you. Relax and allow God to move your heart inside of His.

So grab your Bible and journal and head into your secret place with God.

Day one: "Because I live, you will live, too.... I am in my Father, and that you are in me and I am in you" (John 14:19–20, NCV).

Day two: "But the Helper, the Holy Spirit, whom the Father will send in My name, He will teach you all things, and bring to your remembrance all things that I said to you" (John 14:26, NKJV).

Day three: "For the Lord is always good And ready to receive you. He's so loving that it will amaze you; So kind that it will astound you! And He is so famous for His faithfulness to all! Everyone knows our God can be trusted, Keeping His promises to every generation!" (Psalms 100:5, TPT).

Day four: "Now therefore, I pray, if I have found grace in Your sight, show me now Your way, that I may know You and that I may find grace in Your sight" (Exodus 33:13, NKJV).

Day five: "For I know the thoughts that I think toward you, says the Lord, thoughts of peace and not of evil, to give you a future and a hope" (Jeremiah 29:11, NKJV).

Day six: "Then you will call upon Me and go and pray to Me, and I will listen to you" (Jeremiah 29:12, NKJV).

Day seven: "And you will seek Me and find Me, when you search for Me with all your heart" (Jeremiah 29:13, NKJV).

Congratulations, you have completed the first week! Your heart must be full of victory as you have diligently sought the Lord. Pray for greater revelation to be unveiled as you go through Week Two.

Week Two

Day eight: "The Lord is good..." (Nahum 1:7, NKJV).

Day nine: "And so we know the love that God has for us, and we trust that love. God is love. Those who live in love live in God, and God lives in them" (1 John 4:16, NCV).

Day ten: "The Lord has appeared...to me, saying: 'Yes, I have loved you with an everlasting love; Therefore with loving kindness I have drawn you'" (Jeremiah 31:3, NKJV).

Day eleven: "Here's how I describe Him: 'He's the Hope that holds me, and the Stronghold to shelter me, The only God for me, and my Great Confidence'"(Psalms 91:2, TPT).

Day twelve: "With my whole heart, with my whole life, And with my innermost being, I bow in wonder and love before You, the Holy God!" (Psalms 103:1, TPT).

Day thirteen: "O my son, give me your heart. May your eyes take delight in following my ways" (Proverbs 23:26, NLT).

Day fourteen: "For all who are led by the Spirit of God are children of God" (Romans 8:14, NLT).

As you complete this second week, I pray you are so encouraged by encountering God that you become even more expectant for the next seven days.

Week Three

Day fifteen: "I saw the Lord sitting on a throne, high and lifted up, and the train of His robe filled the temple" (Isaiah 6:1, NKJV).

Day sixteen: "Holy, holy, holy is the Lord of hosts; The whole earth is full of His glory!" (Isaiah 6:3, NKJV).

Day seventeen: "Then he dreamed, and behold, a ladder was set up on the earth, and its top reached to heaven; and there the angels of God were ascending and descending on it" (Genesis 28:12, NKJV).

Day eighteen: "After these things I looked, and behold, a door standing open in heaven. And the first voice which I heard was like a trumpet speaking with me, saying, 'Come up here, and I will show you things which must take place after this'" (Revelation 4:1, NKJV).

Day nineteen: "And the LORD answered me: 'Write the vision; make it plain on tablets, so he may run who reads it'" (Habakkuk 2:2, ESV).

Day twenty: "Call to Me, and I will answer you, and show you great and mighty things, which you do not know" (Jeremiah 33:3, NKJV).

Day twenty-one: "For still the vision awaits its appointed time; it hastens to the end—it will not lie. If it seems slow, wait for it; it will surely come; it will not delay" (Habakkuk 2:3, ESV).

Three weeks finished! As you enter into Week Four, you may begin to sense a heightened sensitivity to the leading of the Lord and a quicker entry into His presence. Ask the Holy Spirit to heighten your senses to the way He is communicating.

Week Four

Day twenty-two: "No promise from God is empty of power, for with God there is no such thing as impossibility" (Luke 1:37, TPT).

Day twenty-three: "For I will do whatever you ask Me to do when you ask Me in My name. That is how the Son will show what the Father is really like and bring glory to Him" (John 14:13, TPT).

Day twenty-four: "We look away from the natural realm and we fasten our gaze onto Jesus who birthed faith within us and who leads us forward into faith's perfection. His example is this: Because his heart was filled with the joy of knowing that you would be his, he endured the agony of the cross and conquered its humiliation, and now sits exalted at the right hand of the throne of God" (Hebrews 12:2, TPT).

Day twenty-five: "And you know that God anointed Jesus of Nazareth with the Holy Spirit and with power. Then Jesus went around doing good and healing all who were oppressed by the devil, for God was with him" (Acts 10:38, NLT).

Day twenty-six: "The kingdom of heaven is at hand. 'Heal the sick, cleanse the lepers, raise the dead, cast out demons. Freely you have received, freely give'" (Matthew 10:7–8, NKJV).

Day twenty-seven: "Yes, my prayer for you is that every moment you will experience the measureless power of God made available to you through faith. Then your lives will be an advertisement of this immense power as it works through you!" (Ephesians 1:19, TPT).

Day twenty-eight: "Never doubt God's mighty power to work in you and accomplish all this. He will achieve infinitely more than your greatest request, your most unbelievable dream, and exceed your wildest imagination! He will outdo them all, for His miraculous power constantly energizes you!" (Ephesians 3:20, TPT).

As you end Week Four, I pray you will be filled with the confidence in the power God has released in you through His Son. Look for Week Five to bring encounters in confirming His desires for you.

Week Five

Day twenty-nine: "He was transfigured before them. His face shone like the sun, and His clothes became as white as the light" (Matthew 17:2, NKJV).

Day thirty: "I was watching in the night visions, And behold, One like the Son of Man, Coming with the clouds of heaven! He came to the Ancient of Days, And they brought Him near before Him" (Daniel 7:13, NKJV).

Day thirty-one: "And the word of the Lord came to me...saying, 'What do you see?'" (Jeremiah 1:13, NKJV).

Day thirty-two: "The Lord God has given Me The tongue of the learned, That I should know how to speak a word in season to him who is weary. He awakens Me morning by morning, He awakens My ear to hear as the learned" (Isaiah 50:4, NKJV).

Day thirty-three: "Your ears shall hear a word behind you, saying, 'This is the way, walk in it,' Whenever you turn to the right hand or whenever you turn to the left" (Isaiah 30:21, NKJV).

Day thirty-four: "Be careful to obey all these commands I am giving you. Show love to the LORD your God by walking in his ways and holding tightly to him" (Deuteronomy 11:22, NLT).

Day thirty-five: "Then He opens the ears of men, And seals their instruction" (Job 33:16, NKJV).

Closing thirty-five days of encountering His Presence stirs our desire for more. As you begin Week Six, ask the Lord to breathe His full breath into you so you may exhale fullness to others.

Week Six

Day thirty-six: "Draw me into Your heart and lead me out, We will run away together—Into Your cloud-filled chamber!" (Song of Songs 1:4, TPT).

Day thirty-seven: "Arise, shine; For your light has come! And the glory of the Lord is risen upon you" (Isaiah 60:1, NKJV).

Day thirty-eight: "Can you not discern This new day of destiny breaking forth around you? The early sign of My purposes and plans are bursting forth. The budding vines of new life Are now blooming everywhere; The fragrance of their flowers whispers: 'There is change in the air'" (Song of Songs 2:13, TPT).

Day thirty-nine: "Fasten Me upon your heart As a seal of fire forevermore. This living, consuming flame…From the burning heart of God…" (Song of Songs 8:6, TPT).

Day forty: "For I,' says the Lord, 'will be a wall of fire all around her, and I will be the glory in her midst'" (Zechariah 2:5, NKJV).

Day forty-one: "So the cloud of the Lord was over the Holy Tent during the day, and there was a fire in the cloud at night..." (Exodus 0:38, NCV).

Day forty-two: "Yet all day long God's promises of love pour over me. Through the night I sing His songs..." (Psalm 42:8, TPT).

How wonderful is our Mighty God who has faithfully led us through six weeks of His Presence! Be amazed at what He has done! Enjoy this last week, and I pray by the end of this journey, you will see a new essence of God's desire for intimacy with you.

Week Seven

Day forty-three: "When they went, I heard the noise of their wings, like the noise of many waters, like the voice of the Almighty, a tumult like the noise of an army; and when they stood still, they let down their wings" (Ezekiel 1:24, NKJV).

Day forty-four: "Like the appearance of a rainbow in a cloud on a rainy day, so was the appearance of the brightness all around it. This was the appearance of the likeness of the glory of the Lord. So when I saw it, I fell on my face, and I heard a voice of One speaking" (Ezekiel 1:28, NKJV).

Day forty-five: "'Lord, I pray, open his eyes that he may see.' Then the Lord opened the eyes of the young man, and he saw. And behold, the mountain was full of horses and chariots of fire all around…" (2 Kings 6:17, NKJV).

Day forty-six: "The light of God will brighten the eyes of your innermost being, flooding you with light, until you experience the full revelation of our great hope of glory…" (Ephesians 1:18, TPT).

Day forty-seven: "There is a divine mystery—a secret surprise that has been concealed from the world for generations, but now it's being revealed, unfolded and manifested for every holy believer to experience. Living within you is the Christ who floods you with the expectation of glory!" (Colossians 1:26–27, TPT).

Day forty-eight: "So all of us who have had that veil removed can see and reflect the glory of the Lord. And the Lord—who is the Spirit—makes us more and more like him as we are changed into his glorious image" (2 Corinthians 3:18, NLT).

Day forty-nine: "Now to Him who is able to do exceedingly abundantly above all that we ask or think, according to the power that works in us" (Ephesians 3:20, NKJV).

Congratulations and well done!

You have finished the 7-week journey with God!

I encourage you to go back to the beginning of your journal and read the progression of your relationship with the Lord. Ask the Lord to show you shifts in your ability to hear and discern His voice. Journal the things you have learned over these weeks from the Lord and the difference in your relationship before this journey and now. Most importantly, keep the flame going between you and the Lord. He has much more to reveal to you! Press into His heart, pursue Him with all you have, and continue to receive all He has for you! Enjoy the abundant blessings of living life with Him.

My Journey with Jesus

My deep love relationship with Jesus has grown through a process of pursuit and hunger; it was not established with a formula or in an instant. Although some things did happen quickly and instantly, the only real constant is, God always has a way of surprising me, and I love Him for it!

My first surprise was when I was eight years old at church camp. I was in the chapel, standing against the wall on the right side, with my arms open—shaking and crying. I was filled with fear even though I knew it was Jesus's touch causing my reactions. I was so overwhelmed by His Presence, I was unable to engage in the service. I just stood there trying to figure out what to do. I could see the service and hear them inviting others forward, but I was immobilized by what was happening to me.

This encounter changed the course of my life, but not as you would think.

While I was at camp, my grandfather suddenly died. Upon my return home, my salvation encounter was never revealed to my family. I spent years having a secret relationship with Jesus, knowing He was always with me but unable to assimilate the church's view of Jesus with the Jesus I had come to know. My secret relationship was also due in part to the confusion that followed my grandfather's death. He was one of the spiritual pillars of the church, and with his spiritual influence in our home now removed, that left my dad's animosity toward the church, and my mom's "enlightened" mind-set to influence my understanding of God. In all of this, I became conflicted—God was everywhere. He was in the trees, He was in the sky, as my mother professed. While my dad's animosity revealed God's need to control me and take my money.

In my confliction, I spent years searching for the Jesus I had encountered at camp. Once married, I attended church. While serving on committees, teaching VBS, and cooking spaghetti dinners, I struggled to find the real, tangible, and loving God I had met. Then my life hit a crisis.

My best friend, my confidant, the woman who loved me unconditionally, my mom, died at the young age of fifty- nine. To this day, I cherish and love her deeply. She spent the last six years of her life living and traveling with us and enjoying her grandchildren. With her loss, my search intensified. I was desperate to find the truth about God as my mother had come to know.

I began to search for the truth of God. So, I challenged God to prove Himself. I gave Him goals. As a corporate executive, that is what you do. I gave Him a time frame and objectives He had to meet. He had one year to show up and teach me all this stuff, or I was going to quit believing because there were no other options. Even as I write this, I shudder now at what could have been interpreted as arrogance, when in reality, it was my desperation crying out for the living God. I had told God He had one year to show up. I would do my part, which honestly in the beginning was more formulaic than heartfelt.

But what happened next was extraordinary. Since God is faithful, He responded to my passionate pleas. He began to flood me with His Presence— tangible presence! I could feel Him, I could see Him in visions, and I could hear His voice. It was as if all my senses were opened, including to taste and aromas. Trances and insights, prophetic visions and words of knowledge, I was completely undone with His holiness. I had no idea how to define this in the confines of the church. At that time, for me it was "either-or," but no coexistence. At first, my encounters were personal, and then God expanded them for other people. In some encounters, He would give me words to share. I stumbled and stammered as I tried to describe to the person what God had shown me.

He also showed me several people who were going to die when I didn't even know one of them was even sick. That really scared me! He gave me many times the details of a conflict, with exact information of the problem and the wisdom to speak into the situation. At one point, He sent me to pray for a pastor when I wasn't even sure how to pray. Faithfully, the Holy Spirit moved on me, releasing the right words.

I was fortunate to be surrounded with a few mature believers who were instrumental in discipling me through this process. Over the years, they invested, mentored, and helped me to grow and fall deeper in love with the Lord. God has completely turned my life upside down over the past twenty-five years.

God "tricked" me into quitting my career that I spent fifty to sixty hours a week working, traveling, and loving because it gave me my identity. I ended up spending four to five hours each day in His Presence. During those hours, sitting in the park by the lake, I found the Scriptures to be my lifeline—my handbook for all situations. It was as if my eyes had been veiled all these years where I only knew "rules" of God, and then suddenly, His Presence tore the veil, and I encountered the "truth" of God—His love. I became saturated with how much He loved me and so overwhelmed by how unconditional His love was that it washed away all the years of lies which had caused the torment, uncertainty, and brokenness.

God has taught me to journal, recording everything He reveals to me. In the beginning, I carried a notebook, but now I use my computer, and there are times I sketch my ideas on paper. It is important for me to keep His promises in the forefront so I do not forget the abundance of what God has for me.

I wrote this, my first book, *An Invitation to Experience Heaven,* from my journal entries, which included the discoveries I made in my encounters with God over a two- year time frame. It was a fulfillment of a promise He made of publishing books.

This journey has had its share of difficulties too, and the biggest one being my transition from a static relationship with God to more of a fluid-style interaction. Not everyone understood what God was doing in my life, and who can blame them? I did not understand either. Though I was reserved with whom I shared God's move in my life, I was still met with much resistance from those I loved and looked up to.

I was so perplexed, having to have a secret life about Jesus, and the signs and wonders and the truths of the Bible. I could not understand why it was such a problem to talk about it, let alone walk in it. What I had to learn was that many only want God in a palatable bite. Why don't they want all of God? I had finally encountered the Lord I sought for so long. I could not fathom keeping Him a secret. I so wanted to run away as fast as I could, but God would not let me. He called me to stay and honor the place which He put me, and there came a great benefit in my staying as I grew in my dependence and trust in Him.

A well-known prophet said to me as we were visiting a mutual friend. "Something has really come at you ... has tried to really destroy you." And it was true. But Jesus has come to destroy the works of the enemy, and whatever has tried to destroy me, Jesus destroyed for me!

When I saw Jesus, I fell across the steps of the Throne Room, and suddenly, He was sitting on the step as I lay across His lap, totally worn down, broken, and exhausted.

Leaning forward, He began to rub my back, saying, "It really is okay—I have you. You will move for Me."

It was as if He was healing all the hurt and disappointment, and the sadness and sorrow seemed to drift away as He patted my back, soothing me like a child.

"Come see," He said. We both stood, and He led the way.

There was lightness in our steps, joy, laughter, and fun, a loving time together.

Whatever came against me, Jesus conquered! Whatever mistakes I made, Jesus covered!

Whatever needs I had, Jesus met them!

Go after God. Allow Him to take you where He has promised.

No promise from God is empty of power,
for with God there is no such thing as
impossibility. —Luke 1:37 (TPT)

Dr. Cynthia Stewart

As a kid, Cindy Stewart dreamt of becoming a superhero! She became someone who helps others find their champion within. After years of climbing the corporate ladder, serving on boards and owning her own business, she took a break to stay home with her children. She discovered two things: she was afraid of failing and afraid to dream big! Ultimately, her journey to discover her passion included physical well-being, discipline, spiritual growth and healing of the soul (mind, will and emotion). An avid learner, her education is expansive; she also completed a Doctorate in Ministry.

Cindy has a passion for people and helping them to connect to their life purpose, discover their passions and live their dreams. She accomplishes this through many different avenues. She is an

Itinerant Speaker and an Executive Coach. She is also the author of two other books, *Insights for an Abundant Life – Energizing Your life with God's Word* (previously titled *Believing God and Believing His Word*) and *God's Dream for Your Life –Live Your Life without Limits*!

Cindy, along with her husband, Chuck, lead The Gathering Worship Center, which is a part of The Gathering Apostolic Center in Tarpon Springs, FL. Together, they are committed to helping others encounter God and receive His healing touch. Her prophetic heart brings a fresh connection to the Father's love.

She loves spending time with her husband and family. She plays on a competitive tennis league, enjoys running at the park and reading.

You can connect with Cindy, invite her for speaking engagements, or order her books and classes at: cindy@cindy-stewart.com

Her books are available on Amazon.com

Made in the USA
Columbia, SC
11 June 2020